Peace in the House

Peace in the House

Tales from a Yiddish Kitchen

BY

FAYE MOSKOWITZ

David R. Godine · *Publisher*

BOSTON

With love, this book is for the grandkids
Helen Avery Grove
Henry Nicholas Moskowitz
Jonathan David Korns

First published in 2002 by
DAVID R. GODINE · *Publisher*
Post Office Box 450
Jaffrey, New Hampshire 03452
www.godine.com

Some of the pieces in this book, in slightly different form, first
appeared in the following publications:

"Jackson, Michigan, 1930s" and "Kitchen Yiddish," *Moment* Magazine,
Aug. 2000. "Peace in the House," *Prairie Schooner*, Jewish American
Writers Issue, Vol. 71, No. 1. "And Go Seek," *The Sound of Writing II*,
ed. Alan Cheuse (Doubleday, N.Y., 1993). "Miss Bartlett's Quota-
tions," *Victoria* Magazine, Sept. 1995. "The Year I Turned Twenty-
Five," *Poets and Writers* Magazine, 25th Anniversary Issue. "Because I
Could Not Stop for Death," *The Healing Circle: Authors Writing About
Recovery*, eds. Patricia Foster and Mary Swander (Penguin Putnam,
N.Y., 1998). "Spring Break," *Listening to Ourselves*, eds. Alan Cheuse
and Caroline Marshall (Doubleday, N.Y., 1994). "Thrift Shop," *Wig-
wag* Magazine, No. 2, Nov. 1989. "Completo," *Story* Magazine, 2001.

ISBN 1-56792-219-8
LCCN 2002110563

Design and composition by Carl W. Scarbrough

First Edition, 2002
PRINTED IN THE UNITED STATES OF AMERICA

Contents

Miss Bartlett's Quotations

My Story

My cousin Bob sent me the obituary from the *Citizen Patriot*, my hometown newspaper. It tells me my seventh grade English teacher died one night in her sleep. She was ninety-three years old. Strange the perception children have of adults' ages; we all thought she was as old as Lear, the king she introduced us to one spring day toward the end of the semester. Thinking back now, I'm touched to realize Miss Bartlett was barely fifty when she taught us in 1943.

Tiny, slender as a blade of grass in her familiar dark green wool, a clean handkerchief pinned to the meager front, Miss Bartlett waited for us each morning as if it took our presence to bring her into being. Who helped give me the love of learning I try to pass on to my own students? Miss Bartlett certainly did. If my childhood was preparation for a love affair with words, then Miss Bartlett was the matchmaker who paired us for life.

Miss Bartlett had the only all-girl homeroom at

1

West Intermediate. Something about her soft voice and fragile demeanor, the combination delicate as the tatting that edged her handkerchief, made that seem absolutely right in our eyes. Who could imagine Miss Bartlett mixing it up with the loutish seventh grade boys we glimpsed in the hallways, the very same boys who starred in the dramas that pierced our dreams each night? Though I know I dressed like the other girls in blouses with Peter Pan collars and plaid skirts demurely hovering at the knee, I imagine us now as soulful Pre-Raphaelites clustering around Miss Bartlett, our hair flowing, our dresses, white and fluttering banners.

Each Monday morning when we entered our homeroom just before English class, we would find four or five lines written on the blackboard in Miss Bartlett's elegant Palmer Method script. Our first task, even before we recited the Pledge of Allegiance, was to copy the lines into a composition book we kept solely for that purpose. Friday mornings we wrote the lines on clean sheets of loose-leaf paper, evidence that we had learned them "by heart." Passages from the Bible, Shakespeare, Chaucer, verses of Keats and Shelley, Browning, Tennyson, Longfellow and Emerson; I have them still to conjure up when traffic stalls on Connecticut Avenue or sleep refuses to come. "Bartlett's Familiar Quotations," we called them, of course, and even now, I never know when I will open a book and encounter an entire passage that's been buried in my memory, waiting like Sleeping Beauty for my glance to awaken it.

We learned to construct strong paragraphs in Miss Bartlett's class. "Girls," she would say, looking out to the desks where we sat with hands decorously folded in our laps, "You must start with the finest materials. Just as each board must be true and each brick sound when you want a building to last, so each individual word and sentence must be carefully chosen if a paragraph is to inform, persuade and delight." She would turn to the blackboard, the inevitable chalk smudge on the back of the green wool. In an instant, a flock of notes flew among our desks. "A carpenter who is proud of his work," she wrote, "pulls out the crooked nails and smooths the rough boards. You must be willing to revise and edit your writing until you are able to say, 'This is my very best.'" The precious notes tucked in one fist; we copied her words with the other.

When Miss Bartlett read us "Annabel Lee" or "Ozymandias," we squirmed in our seats, blushing, unable to translate the rush of emotion that filled us, unwilling to hear in her trembling voice the echo of our own inchoate longings for beauty. Still, some of us went home as I did and read the passages to ourselves, over and over, until their force blistered the pages with tears we considered our very own secret.

Enchanting as this all sounds, I'm not so numbed by nostalgia that I can't recall the nameless pit-of-the-stomach dread that characterized many of my days at West Intermediate. Miss Bartlett's wizardry couldn't protect me from everything. I studied the popular girls as assiduously as I puzzled out verb tenses, and I don't know what I considered more hopeless: the miracle of awakening one morning as a natural blonde, or the likelihood of my mother with her shameful Yiddish accent being elected president of the PTA.

I never could predict the nature of my betrayal; would it be a telltale blotch at the back of my skirt or some incriminating evidence of the Jewishness I was now determined to hide from my gentile classmates?

Clearly, I was the perfect victim for one of the most exquisite forms of mental torture ever devised by adolescents: the slam book. Ruth Mary, our class trend setter, brought the first to school, a small brown spiral notebook in which she had lettered the names of each girl in class, one to a page. With the herding instinct typical of teens, we soon all carried our own slam books. The idea was as simple and potentially cruel as childhood itself. You exchanged books and pronounced judgment, as terse and flowery as you wished, on each person's page.

When Miss Bartlett showed us how to diagram sentences, we furtively slipped the slam books under our desks, past woolen, corduroy or cotton covered knees where they rested until the next time she turned toward the board, and we could slip the little notebooks behind our grammars. While she was establishing rhetorical skills, we were establishing social hierarchies, and the miracle is for all the worrying I did about the dreary "OKs" that peppered the pages marked with my name, I still can rattle off Miss Bartlett's list of prepositions more quickly than I can recall the birth dates of my own children.

In the wider world outside the red brick walls of West Intermediate, a great world war was raging. "Uncle Sam wants you!" insisted posters plastered everywhere. "A Slip of the Lip Will Sink a Ship," warned others. But I had a private battle to fight. Each triumph in Miss Bartlett's class, each paper I brought home with the precious "A" that seemed to slip so grudgingly from her fountain pen, only served to widen the breach between my parents and me. When my mother spoke to me in Yiddish, I answered pointedly in English. When, with no small show of irony, she addressed me in English, I took it upon myself to correct each flaw of grammar or pronunciation. I was miserable. I wanted "Hubba Hubba" and "Swell" on my slam book pages, and I wanted my parents to speak English just like Miss Bartlett.

And then one day, Miss Bartlett handed each of us girls in her homeroom a handwritten invitation, individually addressed to our parents on square, white envelopes. Miss Ruth Bartlett and the Seventh Grade English Class of West Intermediate School, Jackson, Michigan, were cordially inviting Mr. and Mrs. Aaron Stollman to the May Festival Program. "RSVP," it said, a secret code I cracked with my Webster's *Collegiate*. Of course I knew about the program; we had been rehearsing for weeks: a scene from *Romeo and Juliet*, recitations of "Thanatopsis" and "Evangeline." A few of us, including me, would be reading original poems. It's just that of all the worries besetting me that year, the personal invitation was a turn of events I hadn't reckoned with.

I stuffed the white envelope in my school satchel, already inventing the cataclysm that would explain the unavoidable absence of my mother and dad from the festivities. On my way out of English class that day, Miss Bartlett stopped me. "I do so look forward to meeting your parents, Dear," she said. "They'll be so proud of you; I'm sure nothing will stop them from coming." And so, it seems, Miss Bartlett had yet another lesson to teach me.

I must have driven my parents crazy the night of the program. I can imagine the instructions, the inspections before we finally left our house. That part of the evening is a blur to me. What I do remember is sitting with the other girls in a long row of chairs at the front of our classroom. Our parents sat at our desks; some of the taller fathers stood at the back. I looked at my mother sitting at my desk, her eyes only on me, her hands folded as if she were a student.

I thought back, then, to when I was five and she first took me to McCulloch Elementary. I could recall the skirt and blouse she dressed me in, my new outfit for the High Holy days; the red sweater and matching tam, the wrinkled cotton stockings held up with round garters she called *bagelach*, little bagels. What I could only imagine is the shame she must have felt about her broken English, the shyness about encountering so many strangers: the principal, the school teachers, the other parents, none of them Jewish like us. We walked hand in hand along the quiet neighborhood streets, and when my mother left me that first day, her face was a blur, from her own tears or my own, I cannot say.

We moved back to Detroit shortly after that, and I never saw Miss Bartlett again. Still, I thought of her often when I became a seventh grade English teacher myself, and I think of her even now as I teach writing at my university. Who knows what has become of those girls in that long ago English class? How did their lives turn out? How many of them heard of Miss Bartlett's passing and felt, as I did, that the world she once helped open for us had now suddenly and perceptibly diminished?

Perhaps in the doldrums of February, I will remember how I once tried to imagine what it would be like to be the first teacher to travel in space. But these apple-scented fall days, I think of "Birches," the Robert Frost poem I first encountered in Miss Bartlett's class. "Earth's the right place for love," Frost says. "I don't know where it's likely to go better." I'm happy you went in your sleep, Miss Bartlett. I like to think you were dreaming of fresh faces in a schoolroom and the start of a brand new term.

Learning Yiddish

Not long ago, my husband Jack, started to study
Yiddish again, *mameh loshen*, the mother tongue for
both of us, but one that slipped away from our lives
years before. Though we found ourselves making a
little ceremony of it, waiting until we had the luxury
of a free evening, seating ourselves in the living room
with glasses of wine far from the nearest phone,
when Jack read aloud the simple story in lesson one,
I wasn't prepared for the sudden prick of tears the
words evoked in me. More than sixty years before, I
began to trade *mameh loshen* for English as I needed
to do, but oh, how I have missed the sound of my
first language.

As the Yiddish lessons continue, Jack's reading
to me has become, along with dreams and old pho-
tographs, another key to memories squirreled away
for over half a century. It is as if I have unlocked a
trunk where the words had been stored like wedding linens too precious for everyday use, or velvet

9

draperies, no longer in fashion, but too good to give away.

With each lesson, I uncover another layer of words I didn't know I still possessed and with the words, another cluster of images. One day a counting rhyme my Bobbeh Raisel chanted when I was first learning to speak returned all of a piece: *Ayndel bayndel mit a nogel, vehr set vaynen, demen schlog. Rosh kosh kichelach, panyeh, panyeh, breckalach, sim, krom, oylom.* What were to me once, long forgotten nonsense syllables, brought back my grandmother, the scrub-board scent of Fels-Naphtha soap on her fingers, the feather bed of her bosom, her lap into which I curved as snugly as in the striped canvas sling chairs of our long-ago backyard.

With the familiar sounds of Yiddish, my father and my uncles come back into focus, as they looked in the '30s, in *their* thirties, rocking back and forth on benches in Blaine Schul arguing about politics, making business deals, never losing their place in the prayers, sitting, rising, never stopping until *Zaydeh* frowned and hollered, "*Shah!*" and they shrugged their prayer shawls up over their shoulders and turned back to their black *siddurim*. How young I must have been, resting in the privileged wedge of my father's knees, not yet old enough to be banished to the balcony with the women and growing girls.

And the curses, too, have surfaced like rocks turned up in a freshly plowed furrow. They spewed from my father's lips as easily as the pet names he called me by. No one was safe from that mouth, not even my mother sometimes. The most terrible imprecations he reserved for Hitler and notorious anti-Semites closer to home like Father Charles Coughlin and Gerald L. K. Smith. His sightings or soundings of any of them in the *Forward* or on the radio invariably set my mother to wringing her hands; so much of her time seemed to be devoted to keeping my father calm, his ulcer quiet, but how could she control what poured from the speaker of our Sparton console?

From behind his newspaper, a "Lucky" smoldering in the smoking stand next to his Morris chair, came Daddy's chilling Yiddish: "He should only swing from a gallows!" or the divinely economical, "Let him burst!" Who can remember what other "anti-semeets" were his targets? "Drop dead in a gentile neighborhood," he'd mutter, "Go, with your head buried in the earth and your feet in the cloister!"

As the lessons get more complicated and Jack continues to read aloud to me, I realize more and more how primitive is my own grasp of Yiddish; I recall how, as I moved into the wider world of kindergarten and beyond, I was ashamed of *mameh loshen*; I begged my parents to speak English to me, and so for the most part, the Yiddish words evoke the rhythm of endless days in child-time when clock hands signed a language I couldn't yet translate and our house was given back each morning to women. The visible softening of my mother's shoulders when my father left for work at dawn, the steel edge of "Wait 'til your dad gets home," the subtle surge of electricity when his return approached; my father's absence was the armature on which we shaped our days.

It was in the kitchen in moments stolen from Monday, wash day; Tuesday, ironing, that I first heard women's secrets, great and small, what the men called "wife talk," some confidences so shameful they oozed forth as out of control as sweat beads or the painful urgency of loosening bowels. I'm not sure when I began to cobble together the little dramas of their lives — my mother, my aunts, our neighbors, women from my mother's town of Horodok — lives, some of them, destined to be played out in a language of clenched lips, shrugged shoulders, nail-bitten fingers splayed in resignation on an oil-cloth covered table.

I overheard their confidences long before I understood them, from my vantage point in a corner of my mother's spotless kitchen, nursing a tiny china baby doll tucked in a box emptied of the Diamond Matches with which we lit the pilot on our gas range. My baby, swaddled in a scrap of flannel, lay on soft cotton. I shut her away in the box, slid the box open, shut her away again.

At the kitchen table, among the "everyday" coffee cups, the Pet Milk, the Domino lump sugar tablets, the *kuchen* fragrant with cinnamon, there was laughter along with the tears, of course, washed with an irony that was lost on me until I gradually finished piecing together the stories years later. And there was derision, too, for my mother's discontent was no guarantee of a sympathetic ear for anyone else's *tsores*. Within the confines of her life: cooking, cleaning, caring for her children, my mother, like most of the women she knew, had self-imposed standards, and those who didn't measure up were gossiped about without mercy. "As if I would eat in that house," Ma said one day about a hapless relative who could do nothing right in the opinion of our family's females. "She doesn't even know how to clean a chicken properly; and when she cooks, she sticks her fingers in the pot and licks them. God knows what you could find in her soup!" And the woman sitting opposite my mother clattered her cup into its saucer and shuddered with the exaggerated shoulders of Molly Picon on the Yiddish stage.

There came a time when I graduated from my china baby to the intricacies of cutting paper dolls, beautifully rendered Queen Holden children with cunning outfits for every occasion. We had moved back to Detroit from Jackson by then and I felt my mother begin to take notice of my presence in the kitchen corner A certain way she had of biting her lower lip, an almost imperceptible tilt of her head in my direction was enough to silence the table, but it was too late; the stories I had heard were in my blood, cautionary tales for my growing-up life, models to steer clear of.

The kitchen corner felt too constricting soon enough, and by the time I was old enough to be invited to sit with the women at the table, I disdained the claustrophobic conversations, the skimpy selvages of their narrow lives. I wanted out. Eventually, I married, had children, became the subject of my own stories. Experience and intuition pierced so many myths I had been reared with. But the women: their stories and the kitchen Yiddish in which I first knew them never left me, so I keep discovering more and more. As my own voice continues to grow in timbre and resonance, it seems a betrayal to allow my memories of these silent ones to be swept away like crumbs in a cupped fist and then discarded.

When I first became nimble with scissors, I learned to pleat large sheets of newspaper and cut the shape of half a woman into one edge. If I was patient and followed directions properly, the newsprint accordion unfolded into a row of identical female figures, each holding hands with the next. Once I would have scorned this image, deliberately distancing myself from those who came before me, acknowledging no shadow of myself in what I regarded as diminished lives. Perspectives change. More than half a century of living has taught me to recognize courage where I saw only weakness, indomitability where I saw mere survival. Now I feel willing to take my place in line with those women — my mother, my aunts, their neighbors, their *landsleit* — connected by a handclasp, and not so different from them after all.

Peace in the House

A Neighbor's Story

DETROIT, MICHIGAN, 1930S

To her the memory is always the same: she stands next to the old *zaideh*, where he sits at the deal table, so close she can smell his tobacco and the dried pee drops permeating the front of his heavy work pants. On the table in front of him: halved walnut shells, wrinkled like the tiny balls that hang beneath her baby brother's little thing. "Now watch," her grandfather says, his great bony fingers enveloping the husks. And she tells herself, this time he will not fool me. No matter how quickly his hands fly over the shells, no matter how fast he whirls them under his fingers, this time I will be the winner. Patiently, he lifts the shell to show her the tiny pebble under-neath. "Look, now," he says, "Don't be a stupid girl. Don't fall asleep. Are you ready?" And she nods her head, unaccountably cross, far from the fun of the game's beginning. She tastes wood smoke, dead ashes, sees her grandfather's bottom teeth, kernels of dried yellow corn. Around and around the hands sweep, the shells buried beneath them, her eyes following until suddenly he coughs, and for one flicker they leap to his face; she is caught again. Hopelessly she points to the shell. "Lift it," he says. And, as always, there is nothing.

Outguessing Grossman is a game, too, with the same inevitable results. Meryl tells herself she is on to his tricks, his *shtick*, and each time, gullible still like the child she once was, she swears the outcome will be different. Today she hears him climbing the stairs to their flat from the Hebrew School. Classes are dismissed early for *Shabbes*; the last bar mitzvah boy has gone home, and Grossman will be wanting his dinner.

After almost twenty years with him she can discern the quality of his mood from the sounds his shoes make on the squeaking treads: a certain kind of thump, and she knows that devil, Yankel, has mouthed off at him again; another thump: Moishe with the snot nose has failed to bring in his tuition for a change. She has even learned the staccato accompaniment to the rare good days when he will mount the stairs full of grandiose plans that never come off: replacing the icebox with a refrigerator, for instance, or enlarging the *cheder*, or, perhaps, taking her to Mount Clemons for the baths.

Whatever his mood, Grossman expects to find her in the kitchen, so now she smooths her soiled apron and hurries from the dining room to stand at the gas range, stirring the chicken soup gently so as not to break up her *knoedlach*. Daniel and Shirley have the sense to be anywhere their father is not, especially when the message tapped out on the stairs is trouble.

"Come, eat," Meryl says. Dealing with Grossman on a good day is like walking on knives, and today the news from the stairs is not good. "Don't be a nag," the *Bintel Brief* advises. "Keep peace in the house." She will not speak of the overcoat he refuses to put on in spite of the icicles outside the kitchen window. She will not remind him that even the few steps from the door of the *cheder* to their flat are enough to chill a person to the bone. If he wants to get pneumonia, that's his business, although God knows, it is she who will be running with the mustard plasters and whipping up the *gogol-mogols* to soothe his sore throat.

Perhaps he will notice how pretty the dining room table looks, set with the rose-sprigged china she has collected, piece by piece, on Dish Night at the movies. She has even placed the silverware, forks to the left and knife and spoon to the right the way Shirley showed her from Home Economics at school. Keep a pleasant atmosphere in the home, the *Bintel Brief* counsels. You would have thought Grossman came from Krakow, the airs he puts on, instead of some muddy village, but fine, let him play that game; what did it cost her?

Somehow Meryl has found time, too, to scour away the rust stains in the porcelain sink and carry

down the leaking garbage bag herself without waiting for Daniel. Grossman can call her a *shlump* and
complain about her housekeeping, but, as she
pointed out in one of her letters, who could do
more than she does? Without her help, the school
would never be able to take on the extra pupils that
keep a bit of meat in the borscht. Without her to
divert Grossman's wrath, what parent, no matter
how dedicated to assuring himself of a brilliant bar
mitzvah boy, would put up with tales brought home
of Grossman's black rages, the wild flailing of the
ruler. No, even a man as convinced of his bad luck
as her husband must concede she wasn't such a bad
bargain after all.

Meryl tells Grossman, "Go wash," hoping Shirley
has had the good sense to wipe away the hair comb-
ings she is forever leaving in the bathroom sink.
More likely she has left the comb there, too, and is
mooning around her bedroom as usual. God forbid
she should lend her mother a hand, and Daniel her
genius, where is he? Lying prone between the legs
of the radio listening to one of his programs. Jack
Armstrong, the All American Boy! Even she with
the *tsehockteh* Yiddish her children constantly criti-
cize can follow Jack's adventures. The All American
goy she calls him, driving Daniel into a rage that
would do his father proud. The *Bintel Brief* is filled
with letters from mothers like herself whose sons
waste their time in America on stupid shows when

they should be studying. What does Daniel learn on the radio but "Buy Wheaties"? Corn Flakes are not good enough for him anymore, thank you.

"Daniel, Shirley, come," she says, her voice rising. Grossman is already seated, reaching for the seltzer. One more minute and all her work will be for nothing. She slides a plate of chopped herring in front of him as he rises to pour himself a glass of wine for *Kiddush*. Sidling up behind him, she hastily dabs with the corner of her apron the fat purple drops that have slopped over onto the white tablecloth. "Couldn't you for once take off that *fashtinkener* apron?" Grossman asks.

Meryl is used to him belittling her in front of the children. Better to bite her tongue, she supposes, and refuse to fight back. Peace in the house. Besides, she will not give him the gift of a reaction. As if he needs an excuse to turn on her. Such irony, she had said, far back in her first letter: all the way to America to escape the pogroms, only to go and marry a Cossack. She fumbles at the apron strings, wonders how she could have been stupid enough to leave it on.

Though the letters give her more and more comfort, something else has happened to provide hope, to make her feel less outnumbered in her own house. In the old days, whenever Grossman went into one of his moods, slamming books against the walls, banging the table with his fists so the water glasses rocked, Shirley would glare at her as if her mother alone were to blame for his anger. Meryl and Daniel would sit frozen, unwilling to move until the spell passed for fear Grossman would turn on them, and then there was no telling what he might do. Only Shirley chattered on, flirting with him, tossing her black curls, sharing tidbits with him from her plate.

"Shirley, my pretty girly." That's what Grossman sang to his daughter when she was little, the English R's catching softly in his throat. "Shorely, my pritty gorely." Times like that, his attention deflected, Meryl could almost believe she and the girl were allies, that unlike her mother, Shirley had simply learned the tricks to mollify him. The truth was he and the girl had conspired against her almost from the beginning, and for a long time she felt she had two adversaries to outwit instead of one. But in the end, dear *Bintel Brief*, everyone needs something from someone. The day she came on Shirley at Meyer's Drugs, legs wrapped around the soda fountain stool, eating ice cream from a long silver spoon and holding hands with who knows what pimply-faced boy, a subtle shift in balance occurred. Silence is expensive, and one way or another, her daughter must have known she and her mother were now partners in this business of being a woman.

Grossman lifts the linen *challah* cover and cuts slices of bread for each of them after he says the blessing. On Friday nights he can actually work up tears about the *challah* his mother baked in the old days, but everything changes. Meryl shops for her bread at Ruben's Bakery in the old neighborhood. Like so many things in her life, baking bread demands attention, hours at home she doesn't possess to answer to its needs: the mixing of flour, yeast, oil and salt; peeking under the white dish towel to check on the rising dough where it sits in a bowl near the hissing radiator, then punching it down 'til it lies like an old woman's deflated breast before it makes its ascent again. Still, she writes, she misses the kneading: those moments when, her hands dusted in flour, she worked the dough until it answered the pressure of her fingers, until her own shoulders began to grow elastic with the smooth rocking rhythm.

She has described the bakery where women moil and chatter, *yentas*, all of them; written of how steamy shop windows obscure the chill gray streets, the very clang of the Linwood streetcar, muffled by the rising din inside. But even here — early — plump rounds of coffee cake giving off the scent of cinnamon from between their sweet braids, the clerks reaching into glittering glass cases, still good-natured, joking, the world is a battleground. Meryl is no match for the grim-faced woman, babushka falling forward, who has elbowed her way to the front shouting, "My next; it's my next!" "Pardon me," says another *Yiddeneh*, jostling Meryl with her heavy leatherette shopping bag, "If you don't mind, it's *my* next." In fact, both these women have entered the shop after Meryl, but she is at fault for being such a *schmatte*. She needs to stop dreaming so much; she needs to keep her eyes on the whirling walnut shells. Meryl is surprised at how near the tears are. "Will it ever be my next?" she writes.

Supper is silent except for the clatter of cutlery against china, Grossman noisily downing his chicken soup. Meryl sits at the edge of her chair, ready to leap up to remove the bowls, bring the plates of roast chicken, mashed potatoes, and canned Del Monte peas from the kitchen, replenish the bread, and serve the compote of stewed prunes and apricots that is their dessert. For a moment, she rests her chin in the palm of her hand and looks at the man and the boy and the girl, heads lowered over their plates, and she wonders how she came to be ministering to the needs of these strangers; it seems to her she once had other plans. Then she sees Grossman has tipped his *yarmelke* over his forehead; he is singing *shabbes zmires* in a high-pitched tenor, his teaspoon tapping out the rhythm against her good china cup and saucer. Daniel and Shirley watch in fascination, waiting for the crack to appear.

Meryl is careful not to spare herself in her letters. She tells the story of her courtship without smoothing anything over. She relates how Grossman had been a reluctant suitor and an even more unwilling bridegroom. She still smarts from overhearing years afterward that her brother, Abe, had to shame him into showing up for their wedding. The guests milled around the house for hours, waiting, while the roast chickens grew cold and the ice for the seltzer and pop slowly melted in the zinc washtubs.

Her sister-in-law Sarah, Abe's wife, had been the matchmaker. The moment Grossman first walked into the grocery to buy his bachelor's canned soup and sardines, Sarah had spotted him from behind the counter where she stood wrapped in her white apron. Sarah had no shame. Meryl wasn't getting any younger she was quick to point out, and the truth was, if she didn't marry soon, Sarah feared her sister-in-law would end up living with them forever.

None of this was a surprise to Meryl. The apartment was cramped enough as it was, and no matter how she tried to efface herself, she knew it rankled Sarah each time she and Abe had to close themselves up in their tiny bedroom at night so Meryl could strip the cover off the daybed and go to sleep. After a while, she imagined that even Abe must have noticed how Sarah no longer bothered to muffle the sounds of their lovemaking or their quarrels. The effect was not to make Meryl feel more at home, but rather as if she had become such a fixture, her sensibilities didn't matter any more.

So, Meryl learned later, Sarah made inquiries, engaged Grossman in conversation, discovered he was indeed single and therefore eligible. What was wrong with the match? The man seemed decent enough; his clothes were clean and in good repair despite his solitary state, and when he put his groceries "on the bill," he never failed to pay up at the end of the week. True, he was a Galitzianer; that was a minus, but she knew plenty of Litvaks who seemed less refined than he did. As for looks, well, she would admit he was no Valentino with that belly already riding before him like a wheelbarrow — and his hectic flush: that might mean a temper. *So nu?* Show her a man without drawbacks, and she would show you a cemetery plot. Facts had to be faced: Meryl was no spring chicken. And, most exasperating of all, she hadn't any style. Sarah made no secret of her disdain. Meryl's clothes never seemed to fit right, always a hem crooked or a sweater hiked up in back. Hopeless. Someone else would have made an asset of that thick black hair, but Meryl managed to make even a bob look unfashionable, chopping off the ends herself so they stuck out every which-way. And she was so dreamy, forever pricking her fingers on the sewing machine where she worked attaching belt loops to men's trousers. The last time she bled on a bolt of gray serge, the supervisor docked her pay and threatened to fire her. "I don't think you have a future in the rag business," Sarah told her sister-in-law. "Grab him!"

Grossman took Meryl to the movies, and afterward, Sarah waited up for her. "*So, nu?*" she said.

"Tell me." Meryl can see the scene as she writes: the day bed they sat on, her thigh's flesh still leaping from the walk home in the December cold, the ice between her shoulder blades refusing to thaw. In a corner, the Philco quietly nattered away. "He's nice enough, but I don't feel anything for him," she confided shyly. "Meryleh, dear one," said Sarah, cracking her knuckles, "You see too many moving pictures. Love takes time, and anyway, you can't live on it."

"Well, I don't want to work in a factory all my life," Meryl had replied, "but I'm not ready to get married just yet, either." She wanted to apologize, to say, I know you can't wait to get rid of me, but that would have meant listening to Sarah's denials. Instead, both women sat in silence, so close their knees touched. "This concludes our broadcasting for the day," she heard the Philco say. "This is WJR Detroit." Droplets of steam spritzed from the radiator and fell to the flowered Axminster.

"My God," said Sarah, "It's midnight already. How will I get up for work tomorrow, and even if there are a few hours left, I'll never sleep anyway, you make me so crazy." Meryl's nose was dripping now, from the cold, tears, she didn't know. "I want to go to school and learn more English," she whispered. "Speak up!" Sarah said, deliberately raising her voice. "Now she worries about her brother waking; believe me, he sleeps like a baby. I'm the one who hears it every time you go to the toilet at night. I could toss like a ship for hours and he'd never know it."

"I thought some day I might be a teacher," Meryl said, more loudly, wiping her nose with the small embroidered handkerchief Sarah had tucked in her sleeve earlier, just before Grossman was to arrive. "For God's sake, don't thank me," she had said impatiently. "What will you do if you sneeze? Wipe your nose with your skirt?" At that, they both laughed. Sarah's voice had softened. "That's better. You looked like you were going to a funeral, God forbid." Now she clapped her hands together, and pressed her fingers against her lips. "A teacher? Old maid, you mean. *Gottenu*, who do you think you are anyway — John D. Rockefeller's daughter? How many chances do you think you'll have? Maybe I'm blind, but the last I looked I didn't see a line of millionaires knocking at this door asking for you." She rolled her eyes as if to say, give me patience. "Does he want to see you another time?" "Yes," Meryl said, and that is when she knew she had lost again.

Later, after she has done the dishes and the children have gone to their rooms, Meryl lies in bed next to her husband. He is already snoring, the rich smell of fermented Concord grapes filling the air with each rattle. It's her habit to turn her back to him at night. Willing her body to let go, hoping he will be fooled into thinking she is asleep. There is always the possibility that he will find waking her not worth the bother after all. Though she has no woman friend with whom she is close enough to discuss such things, she knows there are some who don't actually mind that business ... who actually crave it. Doesn't she remember her nights on the daybed and the sounds she couldn't muffle even with her pillow?

And what about the letters? Every time she turns around she sees one in the paper. "Dear *Bintel Brief*: My husband falls into bed like a stone each night. How can I get him to want family relations again?" "Dear *Bintel Brief*: My man deserted me and my small children. I am a young woman still, and I still have thoughts of a physical nature, if you'll excuse me. What can I do to help myself?" Meryl can't imagine feeling that way about her husband. What Grossman did to her: it seemed so far from romance. But that was her own *narishkeit*. Why couldn't she be content with all she did have? If she has learned anything from life and the letters of others, it is that everyone has her own bundle of *tsores*. But still, now that she has begun to write, she feels her particular bundle worthy of attention.

The letters she composes in her mind have become so real to her that on the days the *Bintel Brief* appears in the *Forward*, she can hardly bring herself to open the paper for fear she will find one of her notes there, suddenly materialized for all the world to see, the words scattered like peppercorns over the white page. So powerful have her thoughts become, so driven by yearning, she can almost believe they have found some magical route straight from her heart to New York City.

A small man with delicate bones, refined and learned, only slightly older than herself, a widower, perhaps, or someone who has not yet found a match for his fantasies: this is the *Bintel Brief* adviser Meryl has pieced together from novels and moving pictures. She imagines him in his tiny, cluttered newspaper office, searching for her familiar hand-writing in the blizzard of envelopes on his desk. Who else can I turn to, she writes. You know my history. Tell me what to do. Your eyes are so dark and piercing they could read me as if I were a hero-ine out of Tolstoy. And she blushes. It's her ad-viser's slender wrists that move her most, emerging from spotless white cuffs to end in long aristocratic fingers with nails as glossy as the leaves of a rubber plant. Once or twice she has allowed herself to con-sider such hands roaming her body, a Siberia yet to be explored, she tells him boldly. At this very mo-ment, her husband's great belly rising and falling beside her, she can feel those noble hands on her, grounding the sparks of her electric hair between his palms, absorbing the antic energy that has no-where else to go.

Such *mishegoss*. It's her sisters she blames for fill-ing her head with foolish expectations so long ago, the girls crowded into one bedroom, jumping from bed to bed, hiding under the feather quilts, whispering and shushing and exploding with barely muffled laughter.

They were joking about things she couldn't understand, but still, even in the dark, she could feel her cheeks catch fire. It all seemed wrapped in the toss of a braid drawn across her face in the damp, warm blackness, or a hand reaching up under her night gown to scratch her back. The air hung heavy with their scents: Masha, spicy like cinnamon; Itkeh, wild strawberries; Golda, even as a girl, reeking of onions and stale sweat. A kiss — on the cheek or the fingertips — even the earlobe, like what her sisters meant, like the movies, she can see that — even at times, the other thing. She isn't entirely the kettle of cold water that Grossman claims she is. What would he think if he could read her mind just now. What does he know of her dreams?

There are nights, after he'd done poking at her, after he'd turned his bare ass to her without the decency to pull down his nightshirt, when she would wait for the ripping snores and then creep gingerly from bed. She couldn't sleep until she washed the smell of him from her body. She would draw a glass of hot water from the tap and sitting on the toilet, soap herself and rinse with the water. It was strange: that rubbing with her fingers and the soothing trickle sometimes made her want to pee even if she had just gone a moment before. Then she would have to do the soaping and rinsing all over again to make sure she was really clean. The rough towel to finish between her trembling legs, and she standing there on the black and white tiled floor, her head thrown back, neck arched, eyes closed so she would not be caught spying on the stranger reflected in the mirror of the medicine cabinet door.

This night Meryl is following the advice she has gleaned from the *Bintel Brief*, though she is not really sure she wants to. Peace in the house. She has taken time to bathe and dress herself in a freshly pressed flannel gown. She has smoothed Pond's Cold Cream into her elbows and the backs of her ankles. Like she has seen Carole Lombard do in the movies, seated at her dressing table, she dabs behind her ears from a bottle of toilet water so yellow with age, so concentrated, the smell makes her light-headed. She cannot remember being this nervous on her wedding night, but what did she have the sense to be wary about then?

For a long time she lies listening to his snoring. She needs something from him, something hard to name, but she has begun to think she will die if she doesn't get it. This time, her adviser has told her, *she* must be the awakener. Tonight she will reach down under his nightshirt, force herself to touch that pink snake sleeping lightly in its dark nest ready to strike. Tonight she will be a Biblical heroine, Queen Esther pleading with Ahashuerus, but she expects no golden scepter, and the only life she will bargain for will be her own.

In the end, she has to admit the night is a failure. Despite her preparations and the promptings of her adviser, there has been no arousing Grossman from his insistent stupor. Dear *Bintel Brief*, she writes, lying awake long after she has given up hope. For years now, I have sensed my soul shrinking until I think sometimes I can actually feel it lodged in my chest, a dried lump shriveled as the shell of a walnut. Shameful as it is, I want . . . I want.

Sunday, Meryl carries an armload of costumes down to the *cheder*. For weeks she has been sewing and repairing a rainbow of tunics, sashes and capes for the Purim pageant while Grossman rehearses the older students in the reading of the *Megillah*, the story of Esther. Already giddy with the promise of the holiday, the children are wilder than ever. She is a soft touch and the students know it. She sees spitballs rain like hailstones whenever Grossman turns his back. Even seated in an orderly row with his hands supposedly folded on his desk, a boy will risk a beating to snatch off a *yarmelke* and sap the unfortunate student ahead of him with a walnut knotted in a large handkerchief. Grossman has confiscated a dozen of these makeshift blackjacks in the last few days, and Purim is still a week away. After the hard Michigan winter, keeping order won't get easier as spring flirts and then backs away from her promise.

In the patch of melting snow out-back of the flat, black dirt has begun to appear, and with it, the tin cans and bones dropped there by slovenly apartment tenants across the alley who still think they live on Hastings Street.

Meryl considers which of the youngest pupils she can persuade to take the two female roles. She won't even bother to ask any of the older boys for whom every other word is "sissy." Though she, herself, played at being Queen Esther a couple of nights before, it is Vashti she really feels closest to, the stubborn queen who defied her King and refused to dance for his guests. She always wonders if Vashti might have been feeling tired that fateful night; perhaps it had been her time of the month and she just didn't feel up to parading her body in front of a band of rowdy drunks.

Now Meryl indicates the small chalkboard wobbling on its stand. "*Bo, ba, beh,*" she says, touching each consonant and vowel with her pointer. "*Bo, ba, beh,*" the children repeat. She has appropriated a corner at the back of the classroom for her handful of students, seating them with their backs to Grossman who terrifies them and the older boys whose bad example they will soon enough follow. "*Lo, la, leh, mo, ma, meh.*" The warm room, the rhythmic chanting, her own troubled sleep the previous weekend, and Meryl snaps her head back on her neck; she has been nodding. And then, she becomes aware that her voice is the only sound in a room grown suddenly still.

Meryl turns to see one of the bigger boys — Yaacov it is — hunched in his seat, arms crossed in front to protect his face. Grossman looms over him, cracking the thick pointer down on his head, his shoulders, any place he can land a blow. When the stick breaks, Grossman brandishes the useless half, pulls the boy to his feet by his sweater, and begins to slap his face methodically, first one side and then the other. Meryl's children have turned in their seats to watch, eyes large as Gold Eagles. Mottke, her youngest pupil, scarcely five, begins to cry silently, slimy trails running from his nose. The older boys have buried their faces in their Hebrew books, quiet for once.

Meryl has been an actor in this scene before. She knows the role she plays, has studied it hard. Sometimes she improvises, but, as at this moment, she never strays too far from the text. Heart leaping, with both hands outsplayed, she encircles her husband's flailing arm. So wicked is the force of its thrashing that her heels are lifted from the wooden floor. She says, "Grossman, for God's sake, stop it; have pity, the boy's sorry," but now her husband turns on her, his upper lip gone white, his eyes filled with blood. She has time to wonder just whose face he is seeing before him, and then, dropping the pointer, he drives his fist into her open mouth.

Later, Meryl sits in the front room holding a blood-soaked dish towel filled with chipped ice to her swollen jaw. Thank God for Shirley who came down and sat with her pupils and told them the story of Purim, though heaven knows, they knew it word for word by now. They would have another story to tell their parents when they got home, that was for certain. And once in the parents' mouths, everybody in town would soon know that Grossman, the Hebrew teacher, had beat up on his wife in front of the whole school.

Grossman wanders around the kitchen banging pots and pans for her benefit: an announcement to all that he is getting his own dinner. Meryl is tempted to say, wait, I'll do it, just let me rest here another moment, but she is not quite sure she can find the proper tone for these words yet. What she wants to say to him about the food and everything else is choke on it.

There will be time, when her pulses stop pounding in her ears, when her mouth is no longer filled with blood, for the old lines, the apologies, an opportunity to explain that she was not questioning his authority, only worried about the school, their reputation, on and on. She will say she is sorry to have shamed him in front of his students. She knows she has made it more difficult to control them from now on. And so forth.

Shirley brings in a fresh towel, a glass of water.

She sits opposite her mother on the edge of the davenport, biting at the nail of her little finger. The girl has made a show of drawing the water from the bathroom tap so as not to be in the same room with her father. Shirley, my pretty girly. "You think he doesn't feel bad?" Meryl says gingerly through lips puffed as if on yeast. "You know those boys — wild animals; they make him *meshugge*. Go, Mameleh, for my sake. Fix him something to eat. Don't be mad."

And when the girl goes, reluctantly, to the kitchen, Meryl writes: What legacy do I leave my daughter, Dear *Bintel Brief*? What is the price of peace in the house? And Daniel? What words for a son who cannot protect his mother? Daniel says, "Ma, can I turn on my programs?" He stands across the room from her, hands in his pockets, jingling change, just like his father. He looks away from her, over her shoulder to the framed dime store photo of FDR hanging on the wall behind her. "I'll make the radio low," he promises, the only indication he can give her that he knows. She is tired of being the comforter. She wishes they would all leave her alone. In a moment, she will get up, be herself again. Just now, she wants a few more minutes to sit quietly, letting cold spread through the dull ache, writing . . . writing.

The Fair

Mother, I remember the night father and I walked home from the fair. I hear his footsteps so certainly I feel I have only to move backwards around a curve to find them turned to stone, forming the designs of flowers like the colored pebbles in the slanted street of old Saint-Paul de Vence.

Each step is so complete; the sound: hard and smooth and circular as the cobblestones under his soles. Like this night at the window, each sound seems to hang for a moment, suspended in the heavy air as if it were a pebble caught in the pocket of a leather sling just before it's whirled away.

Riding on his shoulders, hugging the spotted china dog he won for me, I shut my eyes tightly and see on the inside of my eyelids the fireworks flowers. First a curve of color shoots slant into the sky. Then young girls say, "Ahhh." Their voices arc, a shower of stars; their lovers' arms are shawls around their shoulders. With heart-stopping slowness pistil and stamen, petal and stem burst, blast, bloom color in the black sky. Unsubstantial as spun sugar

37

— a pink cloud on a paper cone, then dissolving sweetness on the tongue.

Now my father's steps grow longer; we hurry past window shades pulled down by crocheted-around loops of bone and everyone asleep. With the steady clip-clop of leather against stone, my eyelids pull down. Mother, I dream you and I are bringing food to where he builds the houses. I hear the ringing of hammers, sometimes in unison, more often in counterpoint, as the blows, original and echo, mingle or sound single in the morning air.

When I wake, hungry for words to say the color and the flowers, perhaps I know already I may never find the language to tell you the fair.

And Go Seek

My Story

That summer, my mother sent me to the shop to
spy on him; of that much I'm certain. I believed
fiercely in balance then, in the justice of division;
"*ibbety, bibbety, sibbety sab, ibbety, bibbety, kinabble.* One
for you and one for me until each nut or stone or
crayon or paper doll had been evenly meted out. So
why did I agree to go? The playground had long
before taught me the civility of "turns," though at
first in my linguistic ignorance, I couldn't understand why there was never any twirling involved.
Perhaps I felt it was finally my mother's turn; my
love for my father had cut her out so many times
before. "He's hiding something; just keep your eyes
open," she told me, and so I did.

Much as I wanted to be fair to both of them, I
knew my mother was right this time, for my father
did hide things. I had discovered a hiding place of
his: their bedroom closet. There, among my mother's cotton house dresses, neatly ironed and glossy

39

with starch, and my father's smoking jacket and good gabardine suit, down on the floor where as a child I paired their sweetly redolent shoes side by side in couples I named for my aunts and uncles, I had recently discovered a treasure out of *Jack and the Beanstalk*. At the back of this closet, my father hid heavy canvas bags of change that he brought home each night after work. Some of the coins were wrapped in different colored cylinders, pink for pennies, green for dimes and so forth, and the rest lay loose in the bottom of the bags, clinking against one another in the most satisfying way. I had never seen so much money at one time before, not even at Hanukkah, and at first I only lifted the bags to feel the heft of the coins.

After a while, I began to take a coin or two in the evening, usually a nickel or a dime. I never kept the money to save it up day by day for something I coveted; by my queer logic of the time that would have been sinful. Instead I spent it the very next day at the candy store where it would take me forever to decide among Mary Janes, wax dolls filled with red or green syrup, jaw breakers, Guess What's, red and black licorice whips or long paper strips of sugary Dots. I knew enough to protect my loot, to holler "No buts" if any of my schoolmates happened to pass me on the street. The problem was I never could eat so much candy myself, no matter how much I wanted to, and I couldn't trust my younger brother not to give me away. So I took the little paper sacks of candy home and put them behind an untacked piece of wooden lattice underneath our front porch. Suddenly, I was hiding something, too.

That summer of 1941 when I was eleven, Gerry Schneider worked at the shop as a bookkeeper. She sat in the dusty office at a yellow deal desk and wrote neat figures in a heavy green clothbound book with *Ledger* printed on the front. When the telephone rang, she turned her slender body in her swivel chair, crossed her legs and answered, "City Iron and Metal," in a kind of little tune. I think that was the part my father liked best, for he often put his head in the door and listened while she quoted prices, so much a hundred for paper, so much for rags, so much for copper or brass. She had a way of reaching down to slip the strap off the back of one of her high-heeled shoes while she leaned forward into the mouthpiece of the phone. I thought perhaps that was the kind of thing my mother wanted me to keep my eyes open about, but fairness or not, I said nothing. I felt as if I finally understood what my mother meant when she spoke about walking on eggshells. No matter how lightly I tried to walk that summer, it seemed as if I were crushing something.

War was everywhere: war that came in jumpy newsreels at the movies or in little square blue envelopes from Europe that made my mother cry and my father and my uncles speak in whispers so we kids wouldn't understand. And endless games of "War" that I played with my brother to keep him quiet in the evenings when my parents were snapping at each other. And "war, war, war," that word I suspected meant Gerry, that word my mother kept saying to him, crying with her hair all uncombed while he rubbed his stomach and didn't answer her.

The fighting war in my house made me think sometimes of the junk car that caught fire once at the shop. Someone had flipped a lighted cigarette into the back seat, my father said, and no matter how many buckets of water we threw on them, the flames smoldered away and then just flared up all over again when we weren't looking. That's how it was with my mother and dad. One minute we were all sitting quietly on the front porch after dinner listening to the radio. I'd have my paper dolls spread out on the bamboo rug while my brother lay on his belly next to me playing with his favorite toy, a wooden milk wagon pulled by a spotted horse. Sometimes, for a little while I would forget to pay attention to them. The bugs kept banging against the screens, and we knew how the mosquitoes would have loved to get in with us, to eat us alive, as my mother would say, but for the moment we were safe. I felt the war was far away. Overseas. Nothing could get to us, not in the United States of America. We were the greatest country in the world. And suddenly my father would jump up and go "Ptooh!"

as though he were spitting at her; he would go inside and slam the screen door. My mother sat fanning herself with a dishtowel, saying, "What does he want from my life?" Then I would swear again to keep my eyes open for those flames that hid themselves so cunningly all over my house.

One day at the shop I sat in the office with Gerry and my dad, drinking a bottle of strawberry pop my father had bought from the cooler at Clara's Diner across the street. Business was slow, and Gerry had been teaching me how to type before my father came in. "Semi-colon, l, k, j," she said. "Close your eyes and try it." The office was hot and dustier than ever so that when I licked the salt off my upper lip, I could taste grit there, along with the sweet strawberry on my tongue. Gerry burped politely into the back of her hand. She and my father both laughed. I kept my eyes open. I knew secrets; I knew how Gerry sprinkled Evening in Paris on a lacy handkerchief that she tucked in her bra. My father leaned over Gerry's shoulder and looked into the ledger. Gerry took her Lady Esther compact from a desk drawer and powdered her nose in the tiny mirror. I could smell the perfume. I said, "Daddy, Gerry is teaching me to type. Look at this: semi-colon, l, k, j," but he kept staring at the ledger or maybe at her eyes in that little mirror, as if I didn't matter at all.

The place we called "the shop" had once been farmland just at the edge of Jackson, and the building in which Gerry had her office was an old barn, still painted red, still sporting a sign painted on one side that said, "Chew Mail Pouch Tobacco." When he wasn't sorting metals in one of the side rooms or working out in the yard where the junk cars were, burning them apart with an acetylene torch and then feeding the pieces into the shear, my father liked to rest his back against a jamb on the loading dock, smoking a cigarette, waiting for some farmer to drive up over the scales with a truck full of scrap.

That's where I spotted him that day after he finally left Gerry's office. He was a slender man, not much taller than I was even then, with high cheek-bones and fine black hair combed straight back, his skin, where it was exposed to the sun, the color of tarnished copper. Though I had my eyes open as wide as they could go, I couldn't tell from the look on his face whether he was hiding anything again or not. "Where inna heck is Taylor?" he mumbled to himself. I needed to prove I was really on his side. I said, "I'll go find him for you, Daddy." My father tossed his cigarette on the wood floor and ground and ground it under his shoe. He said in Jewish, "Why do you always stick to me like a rag to my behind?" And he wasn't joking, and I had no answer.

In the loft of the shop, reachable only by a rickety ladder I had never had the nerve to climb, three or four Polish women sorted rags, their language as un-intelligible to me as if it had been the twittering of the stray sparrows who somehow also found their way up there. The idea of climbing that ladder made me think of Jack again, climbing the beanstalk to prove he wasn't just a foolish boy. I meant to ignore my father who had really hurt my feelings, but the beanstalk reminded me of the ogre and those bags of gold. What right had I to be angry with my father? What if he not only had figured out that I was a spy, but knew about my stealing as well? I didn't know the word "redemption" then, but terrified as I was of falling, of losing my balance, it seemed to me I had no choice but to make the ascent.

At first I climbed only the first few rungs, feeling the rounds of wood on my soles through the canvas shoes I wore, but even three rungs placed me dizzyingly above the wooden floor, far enough up that if I let go, I would surely hurt myself, and then my mother would kill me. You have to know how desperate she must have been in those days for her to deliberately send me to the shop. She never went there herself, and I never found the patience to explain the treasures that lured me there on my own, the endless supplies of books and magazines to read or scraps for doll clothes, and always the possibility of some broken toy my father might make whole for us with what everybody acknowledged as his "golden hands."

My mother was full of warnings: the battery acid would eat through my shoes and start in on my toes for an appetizer, while the baler, she assured me, made no distinction between me and a load of paper. If they wheeled me out, crushed in a bale along with a year's worth of the *Citizen Patriot*, no one would ever be the wiser; I might never be found, and as for the shear, I hadn't limbs enough to satisfy her horror of that monster machine whose shark jaws opened and closed on bumpers and car doors, biting them in half as though they were made of tin foil.

So I backed down the ladder and sat on a stack of magazines, trying to figure out just what to do next. I didn't want to go home to get the third degree from my mother, and my father had made it very clear he'd rather be with Gerry or anyone than me. I looked up at the square of light at the top of the ladder where I could hear the women laughing. Then Taylor's face appeared in the square. "Hey, is that you, Peggy O'Neill?" he said, squinting. "Faygie, not Peggy," I said. His long legs wiggled for a moment, then caught a rung and then another and in a moment he was beside me. He shifted his chaw and spat a brown stream that dampened the dust at our feet. "You're in trouble," I told him. "My dad's looking for you." Folding his skinny body like a carpenter's rule, Taylor sank down next to me. He seemed in no hurry at all. "Thanks for the word from the front, Peggy."

"I'm not kidding," I said. "My dad's really mad,"

and then Taylor began to sing that dumb song he'd been teasing me with ever since I was a kid: "Oh, Peggy O'Neill was a girl who could steal. . ." I never really minded it much before even if I used to pretend I did, but this time I wondered if the words had been prophesy or now, accusation; this time the words made me feel lonely and sad. " 'Taint funny, McGee," I said, just like on the radio. Taylor squirted another rope of tobacco juice, but he didn't sing the song again.

Instead he stood and asked me if I was going up to visit the girls. I guess I had a bit of a crush on Taylor in those days. He was good looking with his blonde, droopy mustache and eyes the color of cigarette smoke. He never went anywhere without a little harmonica tucked in a shirt pocket next to his comb. I most certainly was not going to tell him I was afraid to climb the ladder. Instead I grabbed hold of the sides and made it up the same three rungs and stopped again. Taylor just stood there, watching me.

We heard a burst of laughter from the loft and a scampering like small animals on the floor above our heads. "Do you want a boost?" Taylor asked me. I said, "No, I'm all right," thinking of those people on the playground who offer to push you and then the swing gets too high and you say okay, that's enough, but they just keep on pushing and you think you will go off the seat or fly so high you will just go over the bar. I didn't want that feeling.

Taylor said, "Come on; I'm right behind you." To this day, I can feel his hands on me, his body pressing me against the swaying ladder, can remember him climbing behind me, pushing me where I wasn't sure I wanted to go, and then that flutter, as if a mouse had scurried up between my legs. I held onto one of the uprights, and giddy with fear, slapped out at the air ... at him. When we finally reached the top, I pulled myself up onto the floor and turned around. Taylor was already halfway down the ladder, looking at me, his index finger on his nose forming a cross with his lips.

Three women in kerchiefs and long skirts, burlap bags pinned around their waists, bent to the piles of rags, sorting cottons, woolens, silks, velvets; the materials floating down as silently as ash, and all the while they chirped and twittered in that language I couldn't understand. In the light from one small window, dust motes swirled around us as if we were trapped in a giant snow-dome, and some giant hand had turned us upside down and back again.

For a long time I sat near the top of the ladder, just trying to get my heart to stop flopping. After a while, a memory came to me of how, for years, I half-believed I could fly down the staircase in my house because I had dreamed it so many times, and because the shades of dream and day melded so imperceptibly then, I sometimes could barely restrain myself from hurling my body from the top stair to see if I were awake or sleeping. Now it was clear to me that I had never been able to fly. I couldn't imagine how I would ever get down from that place I once thought I wanted to see. Now I wondered if I ever did get home, just what I would hide from my mother.

Because I Could Not Stop
for Death

My Story

DETROIT, MICHIGAN, 1947
WASHINGTON, D.C., 1996

My mother was a shy woman, modest about her body as women often were in her day, and I scarcely recall ever seeing her fully unclothed. But as she grew more ill, she must have found that modesty a luxury for she began to ask me to help lace up the corset she felt obliged to wear as long as she was able to get dressed in anything but a nightgown and robe.

I was fourteen or fifteen at the time, crazy with concern about what I considered the limits of my own body: the floppy breasts with their inverted nipples, the insistent belly, the outspoken thighs, all of which I hid under long baggy sweaters or over-sized Army surplus shirts. And there she was, her naked body nearing forty, a softer version of my own except for the one searing difference: in the place where her left breast should have been was a thin pillow of flesh; satin scar tissue, still an angry red, forked around it and into her armpit.

Over the next few years, whether willfully or not, I would slowly come to usurp my mother's place in her home. How she felt about that I can only speculate; for my part, I took some satisfaction in my growing status as mother to my two younger brothers and as surrogate "wife" to the father I adored. Among my many relatives, I became known approvingly as "the girl with the golden hands," the one whose mother allowed no one else to touch her.

An army of well-meaning women marched through my house in those days, my aunts Bessie, Bernice, Frieda and my Bobeh Brokhe — clucking, sighing, exchanging meaningful looks, rearranging cupboards and closets so nothing was ever where we thought it might be, filling our refrigerator with covered dishes of food that didn't quite taste like my mother's cooking, food that got shoved to a back shelf by more dishes, food that eventually bloomed with exotic flowers — pink and red and green — and was thrown out to more clucking.

No matter what we called them: maid, cleaning lady, or housekeeper, no one would work for long in a house with so many mistresses. I came to recognize with dread the ever more sullen face, the tray set down on the porcelain sink with too deliberate a clatter, the damp mop wielded like a weapon over the kitchen linoleum: all signs that we would soon be poring over the situations wanted ads once again.

As I had for several previous years, I kept a diary for 1947, my sixteenth year and the final twelve months of my mother's life. When I first opened that red-bound book again after more than forty years, I was stunned to find only a scant handful of references to her illness. Instead, I meticulously record almost daily trips to the butcher shop, the grocer's, the bakery. The many mornings I couldn't bring myself to get up for school are documented. I write about my hopes for an acting career and my growing interest in Zionism. The days go by. I cook corn soup for my brothers' lunch: a can of Premier Cream-style Corn, a can of milk, a lump of butter. My brothers are twelve and six. We eat salami sandwiches washed down with Vernor's Ginger Ale. I attempt to prepare a brisket for my father, "the way he likes it," roasted forever, then sliced and roasted some more so it will fall apart in a gravy of carrots and onions. I take my little brother downtown to the J. L. Hudson Company and stand in line with him for hours to see Western star Bill Boyd, and when we finally reach the white-haired actor in cowboy boots and ten-gallon hat, my brother says, "Was that really Hopalong Cassidy or was it only a dream?" I wash clothes when the latest cleaning lady fails "to show" yet again, check the furnace oil level daily during winter so our house will stay warm. And endlessly, in purple ink and even more purple prose, I examine my relationship to various boy friends with an obsessive scrutiny that breaks my heart today.

For as much as I basked in the approbation of my relatives, I hungered for life as a normal teen-ager. When everyone who counted spent Friday nights at meetings and parties, what was I to do with a mother who might be lying alone, hurting, needing me to take her to the bathroom or simply to talk to? Sometimes my father would stay out until after midnight. How could I blame him for fleeing the sadness of our house? I couldn't face it even in my diary. Toward the end of her life when my mother was heavily sedated, her doctor told me that she was actually "quite comfortable," that she continued to cry out from the memory of pain and nothing else. I took that to be another one of the well-intentioned lies with which we sought to protect one another.

My dilemmas seemed global. How could I keep my mother's condition a secret from the world outside my house, when it was friendship I was seeking, not pity? I was convinced that having a sick mother made me different from other girls at a time in my life when I would have killed for conformity. Nothing was too insignificant for my envy. I even coveted the little wooden nailbrush with which my friend Malcah scrubbed the bathroom sink after we washed our hands at her house. She mustn't forget or her mother would scream, she told me. I saw that tiny brush as an emblem of the distance of my life from hers. My mother had long ago given up sovereignty over such small concerns.

And there was something else: like most girls my age, I wouldn't have deigned to ask my mother's advice about much, but I bitterly resented the illness whose gravity not only diminished the importance of my problems, but closed off the possibilities of questions had I wanted to ask. One afternoon after days of endless consultations with Malcah and any number of unsatisfying shopping expeditions to Hudson's, I snuck into my mother's closet and took a black rayon dress with a bodice embroidered in sequins to wear to a formal party. As if my mother would have denied me the use of that dress. As if she would ever be able to wear it again anyway. Better to simply take it, I figured, than bother a dying woman with anything as frivolous as a decision about a party dress.

Day after day, while my mother was still capable of moving about, she waited in her bedroom for me to come home from school so I could help her undress. In the fashion of the time, a large doll in a black velvet gown sat with skirts spread over a chartreuse taffeta bedcover, a sweet smile fixed forever on her porcelain face. Nearby, my mother's cedar chest stood. Among the embroidered linens from the Old Country, a long brown braid of my mother's hair, glistening with naphthalene, lay coiled like a small animal. In that long-ago room, surrounded by her possessions, I turned my head from the disconcerting image of her mutilated body, her dark sex and the salmon-colored harness with its unyielding bones and long twisted laces ... held my breath so the scents of her in the hollows under her arms, the folds of her skin, the woman smell between her thighs would not invade my dreams.

I managed to bury the memory for years, but it might have been back then that I first came to believe I, too, would have breast cancer one day. If my body and my mother's body so resembled each other, I reasoned, why was the sickness not inevitable? Superstition, a stowaway from the Old Country, had caught a ride in steerage side by side with the brass *shabbes* candlesticks and featherbeds; it lurked at every corner to feed my fatalism. I had ingested old wives' tales along with my Cream of Wheat, and not solely from my Jewish relatives in Detroit. As a child in Jackson, Michigan, I watched a gentile neighbor pick heavy clusters of Concord Blues one fall from an arched trellis that stood between our houses. Suddenly she shivered in the balmy September air. "Someone is walking on my grave," she mumbled, staring past me in the wine-drenched air as if I weren't there at all.

Such a strange thing for that woman to say, I thought and forgot about it until, years after my mother died, I first read W. Somerset Maugham's retelling of a folk tale he named "The Appointment in Samarra." As the story goes, a serving man menaced by the figure of Death in the Baghdad marketplace, begs a horse from his master that he might ride the sixty miles to Samarra, hide from his pursuer and thereby avoid his fate. Later that day the master goes down to the market and asks Death why he threatened the servant.

I can still remember how the story's closing lines caught me unawares with the shocking pain of a trap sprung. "That was not a threatening gesture," Death said, "it was only a start of surprise. I was astonished to see him in Baghdad because I had an appointment with him tonight in Samarra." "Oh," I said, putting down the book, shuddering as the neighbor's words of long before came back to me. "Someone is walking on my grave," I told myself, and of their own accord, my fingers leapt to my left breast. I took the tale as a reminder of how futile it was to try to escape my destiny.

Though I am an educated woman who reads whatever she can get her hands on, I never read about cancer if I could help it. I began going for yearly physical check-ups only late in life and despite my worries, or perhaps because of them (what I don't know won't hurt me), I never practiced self-examination. Occasionally I would run my hands down my breasts in the shower and mutter a prayer when I found no lumps or bumps. I smoked like the proverbial chimney long after my friends all quit, and it wasn't until I turned sixty that I conceded to an annual mammogram and then only because I was bullied into it by my family doctor.

In short, while I fully expected I would get breast cancer one day, I tamped down my fears and simply ignored the prospect as much as I was able. This is not a prescription I would recommend even to my enemies. Some nights when my chronic insomnia provided me no hiding place, I would lie next to my sleeping husband, feeling as alone as it is possible to be, weeping as the drum beat of my anxieties matched my heart's terrified rhythms.

That wasn't the end of it, of course; in the dark, stripped of my defenses, I assumed every mole, every headache, every digestive disturbance was also an indicator of an incurable disease already too far gone for anything but sympathy. All this is not to say I took my self-imposed prospects completely lying down. Like the serving man in the fable, I, too, had a plan to outwit death, and it was devilishly uncomplicated: I would simply keep myself too busy to get sick.

And so, semester after semester, as students fell around me, like flies in the days of Flit — from flu and mono and strep and stress — I maintained my snowy attendance record. "Ah, the youth of today. . ." I would say to anyone who would listen, but, just as my mother had, I always mumbled, "*Keyn eyn ore*," to placate the Evil Eye in case it was hanging around waiting to punish my *chutzpah*. I was everywhere: the consummate wife, mother, grandmother, and friend; teacher, writer, lecturer, doer of good, with a life so slick and seamless, no illness could find purchase on it. After the surgeon announced the malignancy to us, my husband and I left the doctor's office and walked to our car in silence. What is there to say, I thought, my bowels loosening in fear, but then the words came out of my mouth anyway. "I don't have time for this," I told him.

I still find it hard to think of myself as having been "sick." Thanks to mammography and the early detection it provides, to sharp-eyed technicians, wise and able doctors, good fortune, and perhaps, even yes, my dead mother looking out for me somewhere, my cancer was contained and needed only a lumpectomy with follow-up radiation. I never felt unwell for a moment; once or twice I've considered the entire episode akin to a particularly unsettling nightmare with no more aftershock than the usual sense of unease that fades with morning. But, of course, that's fantasy, wishful thinking. Six months after my last radiation treatment — check-up time — I'm just beginning to grab hold of what has happened to my life.

Still, it's not my nature to think too closely about

illness; denial is more my style. I find writing about it even more difficult. As if they were soles on a newly waxed floor, the words stick, come away with a reluctant thwack. Perhaps it's my belief in the magic of language. Even now, I can hardly bring myself to type the word "cancer." When my mother was dying, the name of her illness, for all I knew, might have been "Don't ask," for that was the response whenever anyone inquired.

One day, not long before my mother's death, I heard the rap of her cane through the kitchen ceiling, the signal that she needed my help. By then she could no longer even walk to the bathroom, and I had pretty much relinquished her care to two shifts of visiting nurses. Perhaps they were between shifts because, for the first time in weeks, my mother and I were alone together. Now the green taffeta spread hung folded on a quilt rack at the foot of a metal hospital bed. The doll, banished from my mother's bed, sat on the cedar chest with her velvet skirts fanned out, smiling her sweet, painted smile. I thought of that braid of dead hair underneath her, bits of moth flakes shining in the strands like melting drops of snow. Anything to avoid what lay in the bed. "Faygeleh," my mother said, plucking at a fold in the blankets, smoothing them, trying to make the words casual by the homely gestures. "Tell me something," she said at last. "Do you think I am ever going to get better?" How could I answer her truthfully when I was bound as stubbornly as she was by the complicated deception we were all playing out? I think by then I had guessed she was doomed, but my family's rules allowed for no such admission. Uttering the word might affirm it. I could only say, "Of course, of course, you'll get better," and in doing so help conspire to keep her wrapped more tightly alone inside her fear. She never asked me that question again.

So I grew up considering cancer a word so powerful that like the name for the Almighty, it was best uttered in euphemism. After my surgery, I would drive around with my car windows rolled up, forcing myself to practice saying out loud, "I have cancer; I have cancer," fully expecting at first, to spontaneously combust like Krook, that character out of Dickens' *Bleak House*. The first time I spoke about "the cancer" to my friends, I felt as if the word fluttered in the air above my head for a moment, a banner in the wake of an advertising plane.

I've read and heard so many accounts of lives turned around by bouts with serious illness or perilous situations; no such dramatic changes have occurred for me. So far, I've found no sudden metamorphosis from my old passive there's-not-much-I-can-do-about-sickness-(except ignore it) self into a proactive, assertive patient. Which isn't to say that I'm not working on it.

My OB once gave me an approving, fatherly pat

on the shoulder moments before he ordered the scopolamine that would obliterate all memory of my impending delivery. "She's a good girl," I heard him say, "She never makes waves." I drifted off to la la land on the tides of what I, then, took to be the ultimate compliment. Decades later, true to form, I relied on my internist's referrals and got no second opinions until long after my radiation was completed. I haven't read Dr. Susan Love's *Breast Book* yet, and I'm not sure I will. Though I call myself a feminist, I realize I didn't seek out women doctors for a disease that afflicts mainly women; my internist, my surgeon, my radiologist, and even the oncologist I consulted are all white males, and I hardly gave that fact a thought until well after the fact. So, in a time of need, I fell right back into the familiar patriarchy of my Orthodox Jewish upbringing. "The apple doesn't fall from the tree," as my mother used to say, no matter how many times I tried to correct her.

And, because my diagnosis and the start of a new semester at the university coincided, I also responded to that situation in my typical fashion: I set about ensuring that my normal life would be disrupted as little as possible. Five mornings a week for thirty-three days I went to the hospital for radiation treatments. There, I wrapped myself in a green hospital gown and lay down on a table under a space-age machine that to my mind had the aura and physical dimensions of "Challenger." Some days I imagined it malfunctioning, refusing to stop on its downward trajectory toward my breast, saw myself flattened under it like a cardboard cat out of a Tom and Jerry cartoon. I learned to pull my gown off one shoulder to expose my breast, reach back with my left arm and grasp the bar provided, thereby contorting my upper body into a parody of a provocative pose: Marilyn Monroe in *Some Like It Hot*. But I hadn't time for ironies; by 8:30 I was at my desk at school, another treatment reduced to one more tick on my calendar. To my shame, I'm still driven to boast that I didn't miss a single day's work.

No one but my husband knew of my troubles at first. I saw no reason to worry my children during the preliminary tests, but as the days went on, the silence itself became an issue, something else to ultimately explain and justify. I said nothing to my morning walking partners, and as we headed for the National Cathedral, chatting about our grandchildren or our busy lives or the latest headlines, my secret fell between us like a scrim.

I knew Jack was as frightened as I was, and so, intending to shield him, I foolishly pretended to business as usual, thereby isolating each of us from the comfort of the other. I will tell everyone when I find out this was all a mistake, I promised myself, but by the time the date for surgery was set, I determined that my silence was self-serving. I wasn't sparing the people who loved me from pain. Rather, I was shutting them out of my life, denying them any opportunity they might have to show their concern for me. I was condemning myself to the isolation once imposed on my mother.

One night, a couple of weeks into the radiation, and on the wings of two glasses of white wine, I burst into tears and told my friend Sue that the most awful part about the situation was just having to admit that I was not the strong one, after all. I couldn't deal with how ashamed I was of being sick. "Dey got Chahley," I said, doing my best Marlon Brando impression, laughing, crying, mopping my eyes with a cocktail napkin. It was just so hard to finally admit to a vulnerability that had been my ugly secret for so long.

Today I can look back and find much good in what has happened. I've had my *memento mori*, but I see no reason to keep it constantly in view like those skulls sitting around on tables in the paintings of saints. There's a strange kind of relief in having finally faced what has threatened me for so many years. Like Mersault's father in Camus' *The Stranger* who went to witness every public execution he heard of, I have caught a glimpse of death, and this time at least, I, too, have walked away. For that, I am profoundly grateful.

In some ways, my identification with my mother is deeper than it ever was, for now I can more clearly imagine how alone she must have felt with no permission to speak of her illness and no one in whom she could confide her fears. To speak of it would have been to confirm the worst, and that she was never allowed to do. Most importantly, I've finally learned to stop being angry with her for getting sick, and that lesson has stretched to include forgiveness for myself. I know I'm not to blame for my breast cancer, any more than she was, and if, God forbid, I have a recurrence, it won't be because I brought it on myself. How simple and obvious this all seems, and yet I have had to come so far to reach this understanding. And there's more...

"*Mir zol zein far dir,*" my mother would say when one of us children was sick or hurt, "It should happen to me instead of you." Years ago, when my own son Frank was about five, he became gravely ill with spinal meningitis. For days his small body, limp and feverish, lay curled up on a cot in a closet-sized hospital isolation room. Whatever was happening in our lives then, our ambitions and daily concerns: house, work, even the welfare of our other two children, fell away in the face of our terrible grief. Outwardly, we were on a kind of automatic pilot, Jack and I, asking what we thought were intelligent questions of the doctors, giving out bulletins to anxious relatives, advising each other to eat, get some sleep. Had we been able to step back and look at ourselves, we might have said how proud we were of how well we were "holding up." But one day our pediatrician pulled us out into the hospital corridor and told us that Frank would have to undergo yet another diagnostic procedure, this time a painful spinal tap.

Jack and I both fell apart then; I remember we leaned against opposite walls of that narrow hallway and cried, so devastated we couldn't even touch each other. To see our child suffer so: nothing in our lives had prepared us for such agony. I knew then as I know now that I could have said, *Mir zol zein*, until the end of time, and I would not have been able to absorb one moment of my child's pain. So we both did the one thing we could do; we took turns holding our son in our arms and let him feel the blaze of our love leap like silver lightning from our bodies to his.

That scalding memory has taken its place in my recovery, too. I have seen how moved and sustained I've been by the embrace of family, friends, colleagues and the professionals involved in my getting well. Susan and Ruth set their alarms for an insane hour each weekday so I didn't have to give up my morning walk; Jack took it upon himself to drive me to every radiation session, though I certainly could have gotten there myself; my friend Dan appeared in the hospital anteroom many mornings after my treatments as if he just happened by at 8:30 A.M., waiting to walk me over to the university;

my four children called every day, just to "check in." I felt them all, and so many others, too, gathering me up in a bountiful harvest of compassion. Once or twice I've given a cheer for the girl with the golden hands. I was a good girl, wasn't I? It's easier to say that now.

My cancer was discovered at the close of what had been one of the happiest years of my life. Some months before, almost sixty-five with an unconventional academic career, I had been granted tenure at George Washington University. With tenure came a sabbatical spent reading long, delicious books and writing when I was moved to do it. Jack and I wintered in Florida with the retirees, feeling absurdly young in their midst, exchanging high-fives like the rest of the "snowbirds" whenever we heard a weather report of blizzards back home. I sat in the sun, tried learning to swim, found a saucy new hair color, lost twenty pounds. In short: heaven. Still my mother would have told me that somewhere in those glorious months, I let my guard down, forgot to whisper *keyn eyn ore*, knock on wood. I know better, of course. I know that my calm and joyful year provided sustenance on which to feed during the sadder one that followed.

In the context of illness, the primary meaning of recovery involves returning to a former state of good health, but I see now that my road to wellness has allowed me, or forced me, to recover so much else. In the wake of the cancer, memories long lost, connections never made continue to flood my consciousness. Somewhere in my adolescence, for example, in the years my mother was ill, I formed a friendship with Emily Dickinson that remains to this day. Her enigmatic little poems with their breathtaking first lines enchanted me.

Ours was a three-bedroom house on Burlingame in Detroit; over time we all moved from room to room to accommodate the various stages of my mother's illness. After the night nurses came to stay and my father needed my bed, I hid out in the basement room to which I had been exiled (not without some relief on my part). There I read Dickinson's words, committed them to memory. Though I shut doors and curtained off my space with heavy damask draperies salvaged from the attic, I couldn't drown out the terrible sounds of my mother's crying. Sometimes I sat cross-legged on my chenille spread, rocking back and forth, fingers in my ears, feeling the oil furnace vibrating nearby, while I stubbornly recited Emily's words. Death, an uninvited boarder, a guest at our dinner table, became a familiar part of my lexicon, too, and thanks to Dickinson, a less daunting one.

Not surprisingly, I found myself drawn to other poems about dying. How I squared lying down with kings and my nascent Socialism, I can't recall, but I even deigned to take comfort from "Thanatopsis,"

William Cullen Bryant's poem we were assigned in school. I mourned for A. E. Houseman's rose-lipt maidens and lightfoot lads, seeing in their untimely deaths a shadow of my own mortality. Days when I was feeling particularly sorry for myself, Walter de la Mare's "An Epitaph" could teach me a lesson about mutability, could tear me apart in a peculiarly consoling way: "And when I crumble, who will remember / This lady of the West Country?"

But it was Dickinson I came back to again and again, and for some reason, to the poem that begins, "Because I could not stop for Death––/ he kindly stopped for me––" Perhaps the notion of death as a courtly suitor appealed to my teenaged romanticism; perhaps the personification helped domesticate a state that seemed at the time, so wild and foreign to me. Who knows? I hardly considered the individual words, just let the images wash over me. But lately, those opening lines have returned with a strange insistence. One night, sitting in my darkened study, unable to sleep, I suddenly realized I had been missing the irony in them all along. "Because I could not stop. . ." And I thought of the task of perpetual motion I had set myself once, as if sickness and death wait for the caesuras in our lives, as if we can name the time of our assignation. I understand now that sickness makes no appointments and is not impressed with busy lives or concerned about interrupting them. Sometimes the old clichés hit the nail on the head: you can run, but you can't hide.

So, yes, I have my old life back, and a sweet one it is, but there is a difference now. I'm caring for myself (in both senses of the word), and that means experiencing the time left me — and I pray it's many years — in a slightly different way. My days are as crowded as ever, one stepping on the hem of the next, but I'm trying to spend my hours more deliberately now, as if each were a golden coin, luminous and precious as the full moon. I'm learning to say another new word besides "cancer," and that word is "no." No to people I don't want to see, no to things I don't want to do. And I'm rediscovering the beauty of "yes." Yes to what pleases me; yes to what makes me feel good.

We learned during the Depression never to throw away anything that was still useful. Perhaps the economy was a holdover from frugal days in the Old Country. In any event, there was no disposable society for us. Shopkeepers wrapped bundles in twine that unreeled from a great ball hanging over the counter, and I remember my mother never cut the string when she unwrapped the packages at home. She slipped the string off whole and tossed it into a drawer where the bits and pieces of twine over time formed themselves into a coil as dense as my mother's shorn brown braid. One morning I would come rummaging for a skate-key string or a length of twine for a cat's cradle and then would begin the tedious process of searching for a beginning in all that tangle. But then, we don't call that loose thread a "beginning," do we? Rather it is an "end" we look for. And so it is with my story. What is beginning? What is end? Aren't they, perhaps, both finally the same?

The Year I Turned Twenty-five

My Story

OAK PARK, MICHIGAN, 1956

It's strange about mnemonic devices that engrave certain events in memory. I spent most of my twenty-fourth year pregnant with my third child. Jack and I drove to Lansing for the Democratic inaugural "gala" in January, 1955, celebrating a historic sweep of the state offices. Adlai Stevenson's loss to Eisenhower two years before hung around the festivities like an unwelcome guest, but we were determined to enjoy what victory we could. Perhaps it was the cheap Paw Paw, Michigan, bubbly that did it; for whatever his reasons, Jack took it upon himself to share our news with everyone in earshot. Since I had barely acknowledged my condition to myself, and since the baby wasn't due until August, he thereby sentenced me to what came to feel like the longest pregnancy on record.

We hadn't the term "global warming" as a reference point yet, but the Michigan summer was particularly brutal that year, or so it seemed to me as

71

I grew larger by the hour, and finding something cool to wear became a daily challenge. Central air was still for movie houses then, and for those who didn't know where else to put their money. We sometimes drove out to Belle Isle at night as our parents had done, challenging mosquitoes for a place to sleep on the damp thick grass, lying blanket to blanket with other sweltering families like ourselves.

By early August as my due date approached, I began to let go of the outside world and turned inward the way women often do in late pregnancy. I had all I could do to keep my other two children from killing each other and the heat from killing me. My father, recently married for the third time, bought his newest wife Detroit's latest: a red and white hard-top Pontiac Star Chief with a slick red vinyl interior. And after my delivery, just so there would be no hard feelings, he drove up to Sinai Hospital, his head barely clearing the steering wheel, to take me and the baby home in an exact duplicate of that racy car. "*Tochter*," he said, handing me the keys while ashes from his Lucky Strike sifted down on me and the baby, "Use it in good health."

The day of the *briss*, the temperature broke all records for August. I remember hiding in my bedroom, surrounded by women friends, my still-swollen body clad in my only decent maternity dress, an outfit I had sworn to incinerate as soon as the baby came. My aunts elbowed each other in and out of our tiny kitchen, preparing platters of bagels and cream cheese, smoked fish with their skins like golden foil, pickled herring, lox the soft color of apricots; tuna and egg salads, cole slaw, raisin-studded coffee cakes and *eier kichel*, light as dandelion puff.

Standing on our withering front lawn, the men mopped their perspiring faces with big white handkerchiefs and jingled their keys in damp pockets. We were waiting for the *mohel* who was doing a land office circumcision business in our subdivision, for nothing could stop the babies, not the Cold War, or closer to our lives, the *Life* magazine photos reminding us that all over America, school children crouched under their desks with their hands cradling their heads, practicing what to do in the event of an atomic bomb attack. It appeared that, like Jack and me, couples were determined to produce the four children that would help repopulate the world with our own kind.

Meanwhile, the guest of honor slept peacefully in my arms, dressed in a tiny white batiste romper whose scalloped collar had been embroidered with blue flowers, somewhere in the Philippines. And a distant island is exactly where I wished we both were the moment I reluctantly handed him over to his godmother who carried him into the living room on a lacy, white pillow.

Only one incident from that afternoon took root in the crevices of my memory, burrowing down the way such things will do with the tenacity that can later crack concrete. My friend Rosemary who had never attended a *briss* before, watched the proceedings with keen interest from a large wing chair close to where the *mohel* stood, his glittering surgical instruments laid out on a table. She could afford to take a scientific interest; after all, it wasn't her son lying on that pillow.

After the ritual was over, after the men had downed their celebratory Scotch and the women began serving the food, after my son was safely back in my arms sucking on a bit of cloth soaked in wine, my Uncle Itzel, who years before had discovered a more direct route to the spirits, approached Rosemary in the wing chair where she still sat dressed in a festive white dress. He planted a wet kiss on her cheek and said, "Mazel tov, Dollink; may your son live to a hundred and twenty, and may you and your husband have much naches from him!" Then Uncle Itzel pressed something into Rosemary's surprised palm. "That was the part of the ceremony I liked best," she told me later as she handed over the money. I still remember the sum because it was a handsome gift for those days, and because the three crisp bills Uncle Itzel had mistakenly given Rosemary added up to twenty-five, the birthday I had observed only two weeks before.

Spring Break

An Invention

Of course I knew you right away, Laura: the long, straight lemon yellow hair, raggedy jeans and tattered leather sandals, the T-shirt that announced your latest cause, the same breasts and hips that had cars rear-ending each other on Connecticut Avenue when you were only twelve. And what could you be now? Seventeen, if that. It's been years since you ran away from home to hitchhike across the country, one of those kids who needed to get lost to find herself. After your parents hired the detectives to bring you home, you came back to school for a little while, back to my eighth grade English class where you wrote poems about unicorns and shimmering butterflies and crystal tears, nothing that could give me a clue as to what you had encountered on that crazy journey.

Not long after your return, you locked yourself in one of the stalls in the girl's lavatory. Do you remember that? When they sent for me as someone who might get through to you, I stood there like an idiot, feeling no more capable of piercing your wall of silence than I could the seamless Formica door that hid you. And why should you talk to me? What language would we use? Who could translate for me the "joints" and "weed" and "nickel bags?" In what dictionary would I find the coupling you discovered at half my age?

Perhaps what we needed to pass back and forth was beyond speech. No great matter. I waved away the curious glances of the other girls, finally emptied the washroom of all but the two of us. When you persisted in your silence, I thought for a moment of getting down on my belly and crawling under the stall door. In the end, worried as I was, I hadn't the conviction to do it. Whatever you were considering in that makeshift privacy you had created, I fiercely believed I had no right to violate it. So I leaned against a wash basin and said, "Laura, please come out." And finally, why, you never said, you did open the door and let me put my arms around your unyielding shoulders.

You sat there in my office and spoke in initials. You said D-and-C, IUD, never the other word that hung like an electric fence between us. I tried to be calm; I smiled the way teachers do today at all sorts of secrets. I smiled for fear my horror would drive you away from me, would constitute one more betrayal for you in a world where foundations rock so soon. Small ironies pervaded the room like chalk dust; in a strange way, your would-be counselor felt she knew less of life than you did. In fact, I coveted your seeming composure, respected you for having the decency to tremble a little now that it was done. What could it have been like for you to have people poking around inside you?

You sat there, your hair a dim shadow on the rose-magenta silk I had hung the fall before when school began. Outside the snow fell perversely on tight round buds. Make a tiny snowball and push it with the palm of your hand, soft, soft over the ground. Now it gathers more snow to itself, and soon, the ball is heavy and hard to push. Two hands and all your body to push until the great round icy thing strips the ground to bare, black earth and still you push and still it gathers.

For weeks the teacher's lounge talked of nothing but you — in the end I had to tell the secret. At faculty meetings, you topped the agenda. What were we to do with you? We felt tongue-tied around you, as if what you had experienced so early set you apart from all of us. We didn't know how to connect to you, Baby-Woman. Some of us were almost ashamed of how being female had betrayed you. Some of us, deep down, blamed your precocious beauty for what had happened, as though you could have cut off those breasts or should have hidden them in dresses shaped like tents. In all that chatter, we couldn't find the words to comfort you ... or ourselves.

Pale and pulled into yourself, you came to school, your homework done in a round hand, tiny hearts over the i's and at the ends of sentences. I remember the lunches you would bring in an English biscuit tin printed all in flowers: thin slices of roast beef, bloody at the core, with a small container of hollandaise; giant strawberries, out of season; artichokes you plucked, leaf by leaf, and drew through your sharp little teeth.

Then you stopped coming again. Your father emptied your locker of papers and announcements you had never taken home, gym shorts and shoes, an umbrella, a small Teddy bear in a University of Maryland T-shirt. He looked down at the floor, your father, a little man dressed in a blue work shirt and jeans, a silver and turquoise belt buckle winking like a cloudy blue eye. He said, "I've given up on her." "You can't say that," I told him. "People don't write off thirteen-year-olds." "I'm used up," he said. "I haven't anything left."

Last week you were sitting in my office when I came out of class, an infant slung on your hip as casually as if it were a bookbag. Your familiar smile, worldly and sardonic, now struck me as triumphant, too. But what was the battle and what price the victory; you, still little more than a child yourself with a baby of your own, your life on hold now, for years, if not forever.

Oh, I've kept track of you all this time. I knew

about the psychiatric ward. (It was one way to keep you in your place.) And we all saw the "Style" piece in the *Post* on the children's advocate who finally managed to free you. I'd heard your former classmates, seniors now, gossiping about the group home in Pennsylvania where you had gone to live when you dropped out of boarding school. Still, I was surprised to see you after so long, sitting in my swivel chair with the bemused look of a hippie Madonna. Once again your ripeness overwhelmed me, your face and limbs without flaw as if they had been poured from a pitcher.

Outside my office, piercing bells marked off the school day; teachers passed, bent on errands; lockers slammed. Did all of this strike you with nostalgia? Probably not. You've always been a kind of loner, not unlike myself, but unlike the way I was, too beautiful, blossoming too early for the other girls, too daunting for an adolescent boy to do anything but dream or lie about.

There were so many questions I wanted to ask you, things I had been pondering so long. When you went cross country that time, the truck driver who picked you up: what was it like to sit beside him, high up in the cab, sliding around on that leather seat? Did you put your hand on his long blue-jeaned thigh to steady yourself; did you rest your head against his shoulder and sleep? How did the world look to you, glancing down on the tops of automobiles, staring into the windows of other trucks at hungry drivers who would eat you up with their startled eyes?

For a long time after you first came back to my class, I imagined truck stops all over America, places where waitresses with their first names embroidered over their hearts, shoveled out eggs and sausages and stacks of toast limp with melted butter, poured refills into heavy china cups. And you there, eating and laughing, your truck driver throwing back his thin shoulders, preening, his gray life made golden by your presence and the envy of the other men.

Was there even one waitress, an older woman, perhaps, in a soiled uniform, sweat crescents under her armpits, who spirited you into the ladies room on some pretext or other to say, "Honey, who is this guy? Do you want me to call someone for you? Do you need some help? How old are you, anyway?" Like as not, the waitresses pursed their lips in disapproval, and mentally stacking tips against debts, found themselves short. Like as not, they thought, I've got troubles of my own — and put you out of their heads. As for me, I never knew my place with you, not mother or sister, no closer to your parents' world than I was to yours.

Once I dreamed it more simply. I thought I might find a few students like the junior high school girl I was myself, someone whose fingers would tremble when she picked up a new book, who judged its heft by the hours of pleasure it would give before it had to end. And for a while, you were that girl. Do you recall the rainy night of the seventh grade party when we stood in the entryway of school surrounded by a sea of opened black umbrellas? "Look," you said, your eyes growing wise with the wonder of connection. "It's just like the funeral scene at the end of *Our Town*." I loved you that moment with an ardor as fierce as anything I've experienced since. But I couldn't save you then as I cannot save you now or get you out of my head, either, in this trip to France, spring break.

I see you everywhere I go, Laura. Sometimes your hair hangs loose, the sun imprisoned in it. Sometimes you capture your hair under a brightly colored scarf, and I can almost feel the heft of it, struggling to escape. French girls are so lovely, swaggering in belted trench coats and deftly knotted silken scarves. I observe them closely as if by studying every line I can somehow refashion my own look and shape it to a new design. I study, but it is not enough. I want to stroke the supple boots clinging to curving legs. What is the lesson of rich leather handbags riding sidesaddle on magnificent shoulders?

I know my trouble. People are always telling me to "loosen up" or to "wing it." I see the looks at school when my colleagues find me making lesson plans long after the workday should be over. I don't know how they get by. I have to be prepared or I might run out of things to do before class ends, and then my nightmare is the kids would run wild, howling and throwing wads of paper and sauntering around the room as if I weren't there at all. You see, much as I love teaching, it's maintaining order I consider my greatest success — or necessity, maybe. Groups of teenagers standing around without purpose frighten me. They're the same all over the world, it seems. Nothing to do with culture. I've seen them in France, gangs, just like the kids back home, like the kids in Georgetown, clustering on a street corner, laughing, laughing, as if for the moment they were in on some monumental joke that only they can understand.

As if my life were not complicated enough, I find the language difficult here, my college French hardly adequate to avoid constant misinterpretation. The newspaper had banner headlines yesterday: *Reagan blessé*. I thought the pope had come to the United States for a visit. So like me to go for the easy meaning. It was hours before I remembered the word *blessé* meant the president had been wounded, and then I couldn't help myself from running to the American Embassy to find out in English what was happening. I suppose that's what made me think of you again. In the end, what can anybody do about anything, so far from home?

In the market, fish lash their tarnished silver tails in galvanized tubs where housewives reach with arms as thick as rolling pins to pick the firmest flesh. Close by stand wooden buckets of discarded entrails. Hit him over the head, for God's sake. Put him out of his misery. I'd get sick cleaning him, running water over his slickness, shucking the rainbows from his skin. *Mama puts him in the pan. Baby eats him like a man.* How does one eat this flopping flesh that won't die even though its brains and guts are gone? You, fish, stiffening in my hand: I only know that I am shaken by your flopping and your adamant refusal to give up your fishy ghost.

I don't sleep well, Laura; I haven't for years. Whenever I lie down, I'm forced to endure endless reruns of my days stretching back as far as my mind can see. Traveling makes it worse, of course, my present clock on foreign time, my memory clock insisting on its own standard. For days now my clock's been stopped at your last visit. Over and over the scene replays itself in slow motion. You reach into your pants pocket and pull out a tiny drawstring bag and a packet of papers the size of a matchbook. You peel off one of the tissues and shake something into it from the pouch. Your baby crawls around on my office floor where I fear she will swallow lost paper clips or poke her eyes out with a ballpoint pen, but you seem not to have these fears. You expertly roll the paper into a cylinder, lick it, twist it at one end. In a moment a pungent scent fills the little room. Laura, I could have lost my job, yet I said nothing. Was that what you wanted from me? What sort of test was this? Did I pass or fail? We shared a common language for such a little while, and now one of us has forgotten how to speak it.

So Laura, how shall I respond? Up the street, that girl is naked under her sweater: gray cashmere, the color of just before a storm. She will keep coming toward me, her breasts, heavy triangles suspended from invisible wires, the nipples keeping the wool one flicker away from the rest of the rounded flesh. In that space, that fraction between flesh and wool, I have lost myself. That distance is my destruction. She, you — the two of you — pull me from pole to pole. You suck my marrow as autumn draws the green out of an arching branch.

Birthday Wishes

My Story

Some time in July, I begin fantasizing about the way I would celebrate my birthday if I had a fistful of fairy tale wishes. Like Emily in *Our Town*, I would like to live some days over again. I tell myself that this time, as Thoreau advised, I'd try to live those days deliberately.

I'd like a summer day in Michigan when I was a child, a musty darkened cottage and outside, my mother in her coolee straw hat, young again, knee-deep in lake water — water so pure the sun shoots though it to dapple cold stones on a wrinkled sand floor. And she would call me from the water, "Faygeleh," that name by which I am no longer known.

I want to feel between my fingers the pale green silk of fresh-picked corn hawked by a peddler from the back of a horse-drawn wagon. Just one more time to suck the tender milk teeth from cobs we dropped in water set to boiling the moment we heard the farmer's raucous cry far down the next street.

I wish I could still go to the Michigan Theater in Jackson for the double feature at a Saturday mati-

nee. What's more, I want a heart-stopping install-
ment of *Buck Rogers* and a *March of Time*, a trave-
logue of exotic places no one I know has ever
visited; cartoons that actually make me laugh, and
previews of movies I can't wait to see. Give me a
washtub full of buttered popcorn and from the Nut
House next door, a little, oily sack of warm cashews,
so hefty it might have been a bag of pirate's gold. I
want Jujubes and Walnettos, and powdery NECCO
Wafers, especially the licorice ones, and best of all,
I want not yet to have learned the meaning of the
word "calorie."

I'd like to feel about Frank Sinatra, just once
more, the way I did when I was a teenager, and his
stray curl and sweet bending notes thrilled me to the
soles of my white bobby sox.

I wish I could walk into old Briggs Stadium again
for the first time — to see what I had imagined for
so long from the radio broadcasts of Harry Heilman
and Ty Tyson: the grass greener than youth itself,
the chalk lines purer than innocence and our snapping flag, a symbol to my child's mind of a country
that could do no wrong.

I wish a politician could inspire me again the way
Adlai Stevenson did when he had only to say the
word "political" to make it sound like a prayer.

Instead, I will settle for what my long-past-middle-
aged wisdom tells me is less ephemeral than the gifts
of fairy tales. I will gather my husband and the chil-

dren around me, and secure in their love, pass another milestone, content that what exists in memory cannot be cancelled by a witches' whim, but remains my gift for a lifetime.

Thrift Shop

My Story

These dwindling days, with summer's heat turned down to simmer, the rolling hills outside of town take on a haze of apricot. In gardens gone slightly blowsy, blazing salvia (Orphan Annie red), strident firethorn and circus-poster zinnias advertise the end of the run: hurry, hurry, hurry! Last few days!

From Highland Place, the narrow tree-lined street where we raised our four children, we can walk down two winding blocks of matronly Victorian houses and through a benign alley to the Metro at Connecticut Avenue. We can mail a letter at the Cleveland Park branch of the P.O. or check out a book at the library. And after I've played Solomon with my summer clothes, I can take the losers to the thrift shop, still wrestling with the sweet uncertainty of whether or not that light-weight cashmere with the hole you can barely notice stays another year or finally goes.

The New to You Thrift Shop, run by a Jewish women's charitable organization, sits above Wingmasters Grill in a long three-story red brick building with arched windows and fanlights of the fashion we here in D.C. call "fake Federal." At the top of a narrow staircase, I'm greeted by a beat-up dressmaker's form and feel a shock of recognition. On the figure is a familiar orange and blue T-shirt with a seven-dollar sale tag. The T-shirt is mine, or was when I brought it in to the shop last spring. Seven bucks, eh? I'm flattered. I don't think I paid that for it new.

I remember Molly from other visits to the thrift shop. With her cropped pewter bob and lived-in face, she is a Golda Meir look-alike. "I know you," she says, shouting, though the room she sits in is small. "You've been here before." I can't tell if that is a salutation or an accusation. The crowded racks of dresses, blouses, suits and coats, row on row of them, shoehorned into what was once the living room of a flat, leave so little space between them, I'm forced to crab-walk to the counter.

Molly eyes my offerings: a brown and beige T-shirt from Casual Corner (when did it ever fit me?); a good black wool skirt with a silk lining, the kind that looked out of fashion before I shortened it and even worse after I let it back down; a red cotton jacket for the cool summer nights that never materialized; a man's blue rayon warm-up jacket, found after a party and never claimed; a pair of new kitchen curtains, a mistake I never got around to exchanging; and dozens of bags for an Electrolux I haven't owned in years.

"Where are we going to put this stuff?" says Molly's partner, Frieda, a twittering gray pigeon of a woman with a sloping bosom and tiny turned out feet. They are volunteers, these two, who spend hours each week coping with the cast-offs that threaten to engulf them, serving customers who are as ill-assorted as the clothing they paw through. I can't place the grizzled man dozing on a wooden bridge chair and wearing an unseasonably heavy blue and green Argyle sweater, though I'm already sweating in the claustrophobic second floor. Perhaps one of the women has left him near the counter, ostensibly to watch the cash register, but he seems to have fallen asleep on the job.

"Leave those boxes alone," Frieda says to the large Jamaican woman examining some folded clothing on the cluttered floor. "I haven't priced them yet. You'll get me all mixed up."

"You know Nordstrom?" says Molly, puffing on a Salem, "I went to walk in there, and I saw a skirt hanging. It was three hundred dollars, and that was on sale!" The word "sale" dissolves in a rusty cough, and she stubs out the cigarette in the dregs of a Styrofoam cup. "Those kinds of prices are scary."

"You want to go into a retail store today, you better have plenty of money," Frieda tells us in an accent that says Brooklyn. Her inky eyes, red-rimmed, seem never to blink. She is a real city pigeon, I decide.

The Jamaican woman pays one dollar for a necklace of white plastic beads the size of walnuts. "Do I get a receipt?" she asks. "Certainly not," says Frieda. "Where do you think you are? Neiman Marcus? We're a charity. Bring something in; we'll give you a tax slip."

"I've got to go," the Jamaican woman announces, although no one seems to be holding her. "My mother's got to have her cataracts done. I can't leave her too long." "No big deal," Frieda tells her. "Years ago, when they did mine, you had to wear the patch for two weeks, and they used to put a weight on your head. Nowadays, it's in and out." "Well, my mother's eighty-six," says the Jamaican woman, defensively.

Molly lugs a couple of cartons to the front of the shop and looks out the window onto Connecticut Avenue. "This is a good block," she says. "They know me in the 7–11 down the street. I'm friends with the Indian man in the restaurant. This morning they stole the cash register out of the little animal hospital."

Frieda is sitting beside a glass-topped display case filled with wallets, leather gloves, small evening bags and a cat's cradle of costume jewelry. Purses and scarves spill off the countertop. She is pairing shoes of many colors, all stiletto heels. "What can I tell you, Molly," she says. "This is the nation's capital, and they'll steal anything that isn't nailed down.

Someone has got to step in and get that bag of wind out of the mayor's office. You call this city government? Old people are afraid to walk the streets. It's beginning to be bad for business."

A tall, young man comes in looking for a pair of black suspenders. Molly attempts, unsuccessfully, to sell him a black cummerbund instead. "I'll try you again," he says. A stately woman, dressed completely in white cotton, her hair wrapped in a lofty, tube-shaped headdress, brings in a package of clothing, neatly tied with ribbon. I recognize her as someone I've seen in the Transcendence-Perfection-Bliss of the Beyond gift shop in the next block. "We're not a consignment shop," Frieda warns her.

"I know," says the woman, "I just wanted to make a donation." "What size are you?" asks Frieda, resting her bosom on the counter. "We keep getting these anorexia sizes and nobody will buy them."

When the woman in white leaves, Frieda says, "I've never seen her before. Do you think she's Jewish?" Molly puts down the beaded grandmother-of-the-bride dress she is pricing and looks at her partner as though she has taken leave of her senses. "Frieda," she says, patiently enough, "What kind of Jew wears a *shmatte* like that one on her head?" "I'd like to know where we're going to put this stuff," says Frieda, ignoring her.

The Jamaican lady comes down from the third floor where the men's clothing is. "What do you want for this tie with the spot on it?" "It's all silk, isn't it?" asks Molly. "You know what that will cost you retail?" "I've got five kids," the Jamaican lady says. "I can use anything and everything."

Frieda ties together a pair of gold lamé evening slippers with heels that are lethal weapons. Who wears shoes like that? "How's your neighbor who was so sick?" she asks. "You don't want to know," says Molly, taking a profound drag on her Salem. "There's bad news on that front." "You've got your health, you're blessed," says the Jamaican woman. "Let me knock on wood."

Molly glances over at the old man in the argyle sweater, silent all this time, but awake now, half hidden by the counter, his hands clasped loosely over his wrinkled fly. "Mort," she says, "are you hungry? You want anything?" She fusses with the shirt collar that folds out over his sweater, as if he were not there, and perhaps he is not. I wonder if the sweater came from New to You. I have a vision of an army of old men, scrawny legs in Bermuda shorts, shielding their eyes under perforated caps, walking the Florida beaches, their faltering steps leaving long tracks like the marks of cross-country skis.

When my father died, I cleaned out his closets, piling up the white shirts he had stopped wearing months before in their slippery plastic laundry wrappers. We gave the clothes to a thrift shop — the dowdy ties, kite-shaped; the boxer shorts that unaccountably tore me up (I had forgotten how small he had become); the sports jackets that despite dry cleaning insistently reeked of the cigarettes he was still trying to give up when he finally gave in.

I wonder if Molly will take the argyle sweater back to New to You when the time comes. Outside the sky begins to darken; dusk falls early these days. Frieda shivers and hugs herself. "You grow older; you grow colder," she says in Yiddish. "That's the way it goes."

I'm suddenly tired of the smell of old clothes and memories — the prospect of more recycling coming all too soon. "Come on," Molly says. "Let's put some of these things away before it gets too dark to see."

"Goodbye, ladies," I tell them, turning toward the stairs. Behind me, I hear Frieda sigh. She says, "Molly, I still don't know what we're supposed to do with all this stuff."

The Good in It

My Story

1990s

I remember sitting in my mother's kitchen, so small my feet didn't reach the linoleum. On the porcelain table in front of me groaned a bowl of lumpy oatmeal that seemed to grow like the contents of a fairy tale's magic pudding pot the longer I stared at it. "Ma," I said, "I hate this; I'm not going to eat it." My mother gave me a look that could have wilted the starched collar she was ironing nearby. "*Zindik nischt*," she said. "Count your blessings. Don't you know babies are starving in Europe?"

My mother was raised to believe that no matter how bad things were, someone, somewhere, was in even worse shape. I think she felt that complaining might bring down some darker calamity. I only know that her "Count your blessings" refrain always infuriated me. When I grew older and found more to be unhappy about than unwanted food, I pushed her admonition into a dark corner of my mind. Still, her words were stitched like labels into the fabric of

95

my memory, and I bear them with me, willing or not.

Several years ago I attended a reunion of my father's people in Michigan. We hardly needed the printed-for-the-occasion blue T-shirts to make us a homogeneous group; it was amazing to see how some resemblances among us hadn't been washed out even to the generation of cousins' kids and grandkids. After lunch, my cousin Leah, then ninety, talked about Rubel, the town in Russia-Poland from which many of our parents and grandparents had emigrated in the twenties.

"Our little village was quiet," Leah told us, "with a beautiful river full of fish. We had a spacious house, and all our relatives lived nearby." Behind me Uncle Phil, my father's brother, fiddled with his hearing aid and muttered, "She's dreaming. In spring the mud came to your armpits, and we never had enough to eat." He waved away her words with a flick of his palm. "And what about the Cossacks who murdered her father? They left him hanging from a rafter in the house for everyone to see. That she doesn't mention."

How typical of Leah to have cherished the good things to pass on to us. In truth, her life had been exceedingly hard and was shadowed by tragedy even after she finally reached the United States. Yet through the years she always managed to count blessings even when it seemed to me that no blessings were in sight.

The last time I saw Leah she was in her apartment, lying on a sofa. Her hair, thin from chemotherapy, was tied up in a colorful handkerchief that couldn't distract from how wasted her body had become. "How are you, my darling?" she asked, before I could summon the words to hide my dismay. A cane leaned against the sofa near her feet, and I blurted out something about whether she could still walk or not. Leah gave me a look that could have rivaled my mother's starched-collar-wilter. "Of course I can walk," she said, slowly, painfully pushing herself into a sitting position. To this day, I can't figure out how she managed to lift herself to her feet, but with the help of the cane she did, and hobbled a few steps for good measure. "See," she said, falling heavily back onto the sofa, "it could be a lot worse. Thank God I'm not an invalid!"

What was Leah's secret? How did she and my mother and so many like them manage to add up the good things no matter how meager the pile appeared at times? It's too easy to say that Leah's early years had been so horrific that anything else seemed good by comparison. For every Leah who refuses to be defeated by life, there's a counterpart who is bitter and unable to enjoy the blessings that are available.

Years ago, I was one of those defeated ones. My mother died when I was still in my teens, leaving me with two sad, little brothers and a father who reacted to his loss by marrying one unsuitable woman after another. I married right out of high school, eager to get away from responsibilities at home I felt hardly equipped to carry out. In the small suburban tract house where my first three children were born, I commiserated with other bored, young mothers like myself — all of us unable to see beyond the diapers and dirty dishes that seemed to be our lot. From time to time I did tell myself how lucky I was to have a devoted husband and healthy children, but that didn't ease my misery.

When my mother-in-law was widowed soon after her son and I married, I added her to the list of burdens I resented. On her increasingly frequent visits, I stumbled all over myself to show her what a great wife and mother I was. I angrily scrubbed pots while this lonely woman who wanted to help sat with hands folded, doing nothing.

As it happened, however, I gradually came to realize that I could look at my life from another angle. I didn't have my mother by my side to say "*Zindik nischt*," but whether I realized it or not, I had absorbed her lesson in my bones. It was a sin to squander my blessings by thinking only of what made me unhappy. Years later, my friend Margit told me once that her father, a refugee from the Holocaust, had his own version of "*zindik nischt*." When he was faced with a troubling situation, he would ask himself, "What's the good in it?" Like Cousin Leah, he strove to extract something positive from each experience. In my own way, I think that is what I was trying to do. I'm not really sure what made me begin to stop kvetching about my lot. Maybe it was simply growing up at last.

My mother-in-law eventually came to live with us, and I often railed at her presence. But I came to see the "good in it." Her willing hands freed me from the tyranny of the bottomless ironing basket. When she took the children to the playground, I found time to read a grown-up book, to make an uninterrupted phone call, to consider the world outside my own.

Later Grandma's help enabled me to become involved in volunteer work and political action. I actually began to do something about the state of a world that had been merely the source of my complaints. Focusing on my ability to effect some change, small as it might be, loosened a knot of resentment that had come near to strangling me.

Since those days I've tried to continue looking for the good in trying situations. It doesn't always work, of course. Sometimes my faith wavers; sometimes I simply forget and fall back on old habits, but mostly, I look for possibilities instead of courting roadblocks.

My mother-in-law lived with us for more than thirty years until she died at the age of eighty-six. I had been with her twice as long as I had known my own mother. All four of our children loved her fiercely. They remember Grandma as the one who always had a stash of M&Ms handy, who let them stay up late to watch Perry Mason when she baby-sat, and who, best of all, never told on them. Perhaps blessing counting skips a generation. In any event, my children saw the good in a situation that I came to appreciate only years later.

A while back, my daughter Shoshana, her husband Peter, and their daughter Helen, then six, came to live with us for a few months while they were between houses. Doors slammed and lights were left burning in a home where Jack and I had grown accustomed to quiet coupledom. Instead of a take-out supper or an impulsive trip to a neighborhood restaurant, I once again had to plan meals. We were forever out of bread and milk, and it seemed I was a daily communicant at the supermarket. Does this sound like a complaint?

Well, here's the good in it: I learned firsthand what a fine man my daughter had married, what a loving father he is. Yes, there were more meals to cook, but also more hands to clean up — and Peter shined the pots better than I ever did; he could have given Grandma a run for her money. Shoshana and I put aside some old differences and came to live and work side by side in a rhythm as natural and unassuming as a heartbeat. In exchange for the privacy and silence that returned soon enough, Jack and I had the gift of our dear granddaughter's presence in our daily lives. So, did I remember to count my blessings? Yes, Ma, you bet I did!

The lessons keep coming, and I keep learning. In 2001, Shoshana and I completed our adult bat mitzvah after two years of studying Judaics and Hebrew along with a class of three dozen other women. Our rabbi, Avis Miller, wisely brought us together one last time on the Shabbat morning just before our bat mitzvah service was about to begin. She wanted to help quell the roiling digestive systems, the fluttering hearts. We all sat in a circle and joined hands, and Rabbi Miller asked each of us to testify, to tell the others and ourselves what the experience of studying for bat mitzvah had meant to us.

The early morning passed in a blur for me. Though I know I was brought to tears by the individual stories, what I mostly remember from our circle is waiting for Shoshana. One by one, my bat mitzvah sisters spoke, and still my daughter did not appear. When she did finally rush in, she said ruefully, "I was late to my own wedding." All her life, it seems, I have been waiting for Shoshana. She was born two weeks after her due date and has been struggling to be on time ever since. Each time she is late for a family gathering, I waver between wanting to kill her and worrying that something or someone already has. It sounds as if I'm complaining about her absence from the bat mitzvah circle, but what I mean to talk about is her presence, a presence that never fails to make my heart leap.

Here's the good in it: to have been able to sit

next to her week after week while we read and studied together, to have been there to *kvell* when she
mastered Aleph Beth, to be so near I could reach
out and touch her arm or lean my shoulder against
hers, to have made such an intellectual and spiritual
journey hand-in-hand with my daughter has been
one of God's most gracious gifts to me. So you can
see why, late or not, I look on Shoshana the way I
consider my bat mitzvah . . . a long time coming, but
worth the wait.

Completo: A Triptych

My Story

ONE

The first class railroad compartment from Rome to Chiazzo seemed spacious enough when we gratefully stumbled into it, Jack and I, jet-lagged, grimly schlepping the far-too-heavy bags we had bickered about even before we left the States. I suppose nowadays you'd call that disagreement an "issue." No matter how many times Jack offers it, the raincoat-doubling-as-bathrobe packing advice always depresses me, makes me realize that soon I'll be in unfamiliar territory without my "things." "The junk dealer's daughter," he calls me, and I am, collecting the past's cast-offs like a peddler with his burlap pack. Still, spacious or not, the moment the other couple entered our compartment, asking us in Italian if the two empty seats were free, I felt out-of-breath, felt the air in the room evaporate as if someone had placed a glass dome over us all.

He was a good ten years younger than we were then, fifty or so, grizzled hair edging up his temples, dressed in well-cut tweeds at home on his spare body and fine shoes that shone like the backs of black beetles; she might still have been in her teens, a tulip of a woman, all creamy surface and beautiful proportion. That her companion delighted in her — I could say worshipped her — was clear even from the way his guiding hand trembled on her shoulder, no translation needed. Small wonder I couldn't catch my breath. It seemed to me, a woman three times her age, that she was almost without flaw. Her exotically cut dress, skimming her supple body almost to her fragile ankles, was fashioned of a shimmering cotton sateen in shades of black and gray that dimpled in the sunlight as she arranged herself on the seat opposite him — so he could look at her, he said.

She leaned her head against the seat back and her black hair, barely glancing off her shoulders, swung into place, each filament in harmony with the others. I knew it was rude, but I couldn't help staring; even the cunning brocade box she carried as a handbag, scarcely larger than a pack of cigarettes, fascinated me. Here was a woman who traveled light, and I admit it: I was eaten alive by green-gall jealousy. It seemed to me, then, that in all my life, no man had ever looked at me the way her companion looked at her, not even my husband of forty years who was at that very moment sitting next to her trying to keep his eyes focussed on his *Herald Tribune.*

The pair chattered away in Italian during the expectant bustle that accompanies a train's departure. Officious-looking uniformed men carrying clipboards strode up and down the platform, a whistle shrieked, great wheels lurched prematurely a few times, and we were off. For my part, I rummaged in my purse, checking for my passport one more time, feeling the reassuring bulk of my traveler's checks, all the while castigating myself for being so drawn into their drama. I'm always doing things like that, fantasizing about people I sit next to on the bus, constructing a life from the contents of her supermarket shopping cart for the woman checking out in front of me, wondering how others' lives compare to mine.

And then he spotted it: just under the shadow of the woman's seat, what I had noticed shortly before their arrival. So close it almost brushed the hem of her shift, lay a small dead mouse. I had considered warning them about it, but my lack of Italian and the self-sufficiency of their mutual absorption had put me off, tongue-tied me.

"It's impossible," he said in English, not to her but to me. "It's nothing," I said finally, his disappointment was so keen. "Just a little mouse, harmless now." He waved his hand at me impatiently. "That's not the point. They should have cleaned it up." There was no fixing the situation until he could rouse a conductor. If he sat next to her, the mouse would still be under the chair; if he exchanged places with her, she would have to look at it. He told the young woman — and I realized they must have met only recently — "I usually travel second class, but I wanted everything just right, it being a holiday and so many people travelling." As for me, I turned away from them, no longer able to bear his middle-aged anxiety, too empathetic with his irritable unrealistic desire for everything that affected them to be perfect.

TWO

By the time we board the night train back to Rome, we have the traveling routine down pat. The train is already in the station when we arrive at 10:00 P.M., and our compartment has been made up for sleeping with two facing seats below and two upper bunks. The conductor hands us pillows and blankets and a plastic bag containing two paper items: a "sheet" and a pillow cover.

At this point, Jack does his usual European train number; he leaves me and goes off to the terminal to forage for an English-language newspaper and bottled water. Once again I tell myself that normal people get to the station early enough to take care of that kind of provisioning before they board, but then what do they do for entertainment once they've been seated? Jack has to prove what an experienced and casual traveler he is, while I, the itinerant basket case, drag along enough old emotional baggage to challenge the very real stuff we're dragging. His anxiety is about locating the proper car and getting me and the bundles settled, while I'm afraid he'll wander off and get back too late, and we won't ever find each other again.

Now, I've said I'm not the greatest traveler; as if I don't already have troubles away from what's familiar, I honestly believe I'm spatially challenged. In other words, I can't find my way out of the proverbial paper bag. When I finally decided to matriculate after the youngest of my four children entered kindergarten, I had a choice between two universities, each about ten minutes in different directions from my home in D.C. The family joke is that I chose George Washington because I already knew how to get there. Jack says I can only find my way to two places, the Giant Food Store and my school. He underestimates me. I can actually make it out to my daughter's house in the suburbs, too, though no matter how many times I do it, one moment of inattention and I'm hopelessly lost. Obviously, I'm no help as a navigator on motor trips; even if I could unfold a map in less time than it takes to pass the exit we're looking for, the drawings and symbols would make as much sense to me as do the words in the Italian newspaper someone has left behind in our compartment.

Now, I curse myself for not having made a contingency plan. It's always possible to get separated in a strange place. I should have memorized the name and address of our next hotel. What sick dependency allowed me to travel without foreign currency? If I was so fearful of getting lost, why didn't I have a copy of our itinerary?

I force myself to stay in my seat; I remind myself that this very situation has happened before and Jack always gets back in time. I rehearse fail-safes — American Express, the American Embassy — consider getting off the train so we'll at least be together when it leaves without us. Perhaps I should stay put and wait for Jack who will surely be on the next train to Rome when it arrives in the station at the other end. As well as I think I know him after so many years, I still can't imagine what he would do in my place . . . probably not panic, for one thing. Though the heat has not yet been turned on in our car, my palms are slick; my thighs grow moist under the fabric of my wash-and-wear slacks.

As if disorientation were not enough, there's my language shortfall to contend with. Jack has no problem with tourist speech in any foreign country. He's already hauled out what he thinks passes for Italian, but I'm too much of a snob to do that. My grad school French and German might allow me to decode a *festschrift* or two, but once in Europe, my tongue takes on the quality of a football, leathery and inflexible, my brain, in sympathy, turns to cold oatmeal in the brainpan.

I remember us driving through the French countryside one summer when the windshield of our rented car exploded, throwing piles of glass chunks into our laps. Jack pulled over to a narrow shoulder. Shaken, we decided to abandon our now air-conditioned auto, walk into the next town (pop. 510), find the police station and explain our plight. Explain our plight! My brain started its familiar metamorphosis to mush, the football in my mouth cut off my wind. Jack said, "You will tell them what happened. You're the language expert."

So we trudged along the highway while Renaults and Peugeots whizzed by close enough to ruffle our clothes, and I searched the crannies of my memory for the French word for windshield. Sadly, most French critics discussing the Symbolist Movement, say, or the impact of Existentialism on American Literature find little use for auto parts. Finally I decided if I ever did know the word, it was gone now. I prayed for an English-speaking gendarme. Naturally, we were out of luck. The rosy-cheeked policeman in his ridiculous cap knew far less of my language than I knew of his. After awhile, he shrugged his shoulders and turned his back on us. If he didn't see us, maybe we would go away.

Jack, by this time, had figured to the penny the cost of the French courses I had taken over the years, and was audibly computing the interest. I vowed to restrict my travel to English-speaking countries in the future, but at Jack's insistence I gave my French one last desperate try. "Monsieur," I said, temples throbbing, "The window of my auto is dead." That did it. In exasperation, the gendarme waved his footlong ham sandwich at us (we had interrupted his lunch) and blurted out his entire stock of English: "The weather is fine. Where is the dentist?" With that, he took a long draught from his liter of mineral water, resumed munching, and we were dismissed.

If my useful French is barely there, my Italian is nonexistent. The first time I saw *spaghetti al burro* on a menu, I thought it contained donkey meat. I have to admit that even in my present state, the memory makes me smile. I smoke yet another cigarette, realize that getting off the train is not an option because I'd never be able to carry that entire luggage alone. Terrorists have bombed another train station, or so I gather from a photo in the Italian newspaper; that information doesn't help me, nor does the paperback I can't get into. On the platform, a vendor pushing a heavy cart laden with sandwiches and cold drinks raps on my window. The very idea of food turns the contents of my already churning stomach to butter. I sing to myself, an old calming device. I sing "The Raven" to the tune of "Humoresque." "ONCE uPON a MIDnight DREary..." I make it as far as "the bust of Pallas" before I'm out of my seat; I've got to find Jack.

Meanwhile, someone has slid the outer door of our car shut. My heart is doing flip-flops in a chest as taut as a trampoline, and the door won't yield. When I figure out how to open it, I stand between the cars and lean out into the icy air, scouring the now nearly deserted platform for any figure who might be Jack. Suddenly I hear doors clang all through the train. Below me, a fellow in uniform, his authority buoyed by festoons of gold braid, shouts at me in Italian, "Shut the door, *Signora*." I can't believe this nightmare is finally happening; I keep looking for Jack.

I know all about European trains; you can set your watch by them, even in Italy, and according to the posted schedule we had read earlier, this train is not due to leave for at least seven more minutes. Now my fears are justified. No wonder I've been in such a state: obviously we have boarded the wrong train. Mr. Gold Braid slams the door shut in my face, but I wrestle it open once again. "Is this the train for Rome?" "*Sí, sí.*" "But you're leaving too early." "*Signora...*" "*Mi esposo!*" The dialogue is as witty as an Italian opera. "*Signora*, shut the D O O R!" and I do and go back to my seat muttering, "If this is all a bad dream, why can't I wake up?" The train begins to rock slowly out of the station.

In a few moments, Jack, who has boarded somewhere down the line, slides open the compartment door. He has confronted the Italian lire, the Italian language and the Italian rail system and stood them all down. Why shouldn't he be smiling? "I bought us some sandwiches," he says, "in case we get hungry later on." I'm so relieved to see him (and so ashamed of my panic), I don't say, Don't ever do that to me again. Instead, I nod toward the bundle he carries and say, "Good idea; what kind did you get?"

THREE

Our vacation in Italy is almost over, and we've made it onto the *vaporetto* to Venice, our final destination. A gusty wind, a frigid monotonous downpour and rush hour combine to create a jam on our boat. Naturally, I am convinced it is overloaded and will sink to the bottom of the polluted Grand Canal, a mini-Titanic begging to happen, and I'm not sure Italians observe the convention of women and children first. Would-be passengers, intent on getting home for New Year's, refuse to heed the conductor's pleas and insist on wedging themselves into the *vaporetto*.

Meanwhile, still carrying our heavy bags now augmented by an assortment of souvenirs and gifts in plastic sacks, we are a formidable obstruction for anyone near us seeking to get on or off the boat. Not a person stumbles past us without a derogatory comment about the *bagaglio*. Unaccountably I find myself boiling with rage, and all of my ire is directed against Jack. Forget that most of the luggage is mine. I want him to be as upset and embarrassed about the comments as I am. At this point, the baggage is a given; it is simply there and short of dumping it overboard, which I'm sure Jack would offer to do if I said anything, we're stuck with it. Of course, he has the right attitude; we will never see any of these people again, so what difference does their momentary disapproval make? The difference is it will take me all day to shake it off, while to him the grumbling is of as little consequence as a swarm of midges in summer.

The rain seems to have settled in for the long haul. Venice smells like a damp basement, and I'm so cold that even the concept that somewhere in the world people take central heat for granted is unimaginable to me. By the time we have wandered the streets and neared our *pensione*, I have kissed my toes goodbye. Even Jack has stopped saying the winter equivalent of "It's not the heat; it's the humidity." He buries his head in his shoulders and soldiers on.

We're at the stage we reach in all our trips when we both wonder why we spent so much money to travel so far. Home seems so attractive, every-day life a comfortable blessing. No decisions about where to eat, no prodding of conscience to leave a comfortable room for the Babel of crowded, cold, rainy streets. We miss the kids, our friends, our language, even the *Eyewitness News* with its ubiquitous gurneys wheeling out the night's gunshot victims. But then a passageway, narrow as a constricted artery, suddenly opens onto the Piazza San Marco, that perennial wonder. Dazzled, we smile at one another, remembering why we came. We turn, turn in a circle to lights, shops, façades, statues, domes, towers, dissolving like sugar in the mist and the beating wings of a cloud of pigeons, rising, rising.

Now it's New Year's Eve and true to form I've been worrying for days that we will get nothing to eat if we don't make some arrangements in advance. Perhaps it's already too late, the eleventh hour, so to speak, when I'm convinced everything decent will be full anyway. Our reactions represent a perfect picture of our personality differences. The pessimist (me) is certain we are closed out. The optimist (Jack) believes that in all of Venice he will surely find some establishment that is waiting for our business.

So we talk and we talk and I play him like a wily fisherman seeking to outsmart the old man of the sea. Don't push him too hard; he will resist out of sheer stubbornness. Don't show him how anxious you are; he will rebel in order to show how very cool he can be in the face of all this. Somehow I manage to walk the wire with some degree of balance for a change, because Jack does agree to make a reservation at a little restaurant near the Rialto, or rather, I, for once appreciating his uncertainty in the face of all those language stone walls, tell the lady at the other end of the phone, "*Due* reservations, eight o'clock, *otto*." When she asks our name, I'm simply not up to starting in with "Moskowitz." Discretion is the better part of valor. I give her the name of our hotel instead.

We take a nap then, both of us drowning in deep sleep, barely able to rouse ourselves until after 7:00. Then I do begin to nag, just a little, as Jack continues to lie in bed. "I may never get up," he says, burrowing further under the blankets. A surreptitious glance at my watch shows the hands tending none too slowly toward 8:00. Who knows where the restaurant really is or how long we might wander the labyrinthine streets before we find it?

Finally dressed, we head out of the *pensione*, Jack determined not to be rushed, and I certain the restaurant will give up our places if we don't arrive in time. We loll along, looking in the windows of trattorias framed in strings of colored lights, reading San Silvestre menus, but making our way in the direction of the Rialto. Jack indicates that he hasn't reached a final decision and certainly implies that it's a buyer's market, that the choice of a place to eat, even at 8:00 on New Year's Eve is still his to make.

Meanwhile the narrow alleys teem with locals buying last-minute food from bins piled high with oranges, pineapples, apples, artichokes, fennel. Some carefully carry white cake boxes tied in gold ribbon, a gift perhaps for the hosts who will feed them dinner. Some amble with no apparent destination in mind in the way of those who have no concern about where their next meal is coming from. Others seem to be striding purposefully, probably to tables at gourmet restaurants they had reserved in July. Jack inquires at some of the more festive-looking spots where black-suited waiters ready themselves for the evening's onslaught of diners. The salutary effect of warm blasts of air, redolent with spices and the charred scent of grilling meats is snuffed out by the apologetic smile, the shoulder shrug. "*Completo, completo.*"

No surprise: by the time we arrive at our destination, the motherly-looking proprietress of the tiny restaurant waves us away with what has by now become a familiar litany. "*Completo,*" she says, and seeing that we are Americans, "We are complete." I say patiently, "Reservation. Pensione Accademia." "Oh" she replies, pointing to her watch, "*Otto, otto.*" "What does she say?" Jack asks. "She's full," I tell him, savoring my bitter victory. For a change, what I've worried about has come true. "We got here too late," and I turn away from him, struggling not to look triumphant.

Then we have it, the blow-up of the trip, in the middle of jostling crowds of people, many of them like us, the hour growing late — without a place to eat on this holiday night. It would have taken a true Christian not to say I told you so, and despite the Annunciations and Assumptions and Ascensions I had assimilated in the days previous, I have not yet been nominated for sainthood. I allow myself a few caustic remarks before we hit the flash point. "Go back to the hotel," Jack says. "If you're going to be that way, take a taxi and go back. I'll find something myself."

And so, I push him, both palms flat against his chest, and I say, "Damn you, I don't want to go back to the hotel. I don't want to ruin the evening, either. I just want you to admit, for once, that maybe, just maybe, I was right and you were wrong." And having said that, I've been married long enough to know this is not the time to press an advantage; it's time for me to chill.

We set out silently in a wretched search for any place that is not *completo*. The hole-in-the-wall which we finally hit on is terribly overpriced, and though we try our best to salvage a bit of the evening, neither the flimsy paper hats nor the packets of tiny Styrofoam confetti balls can lift the cloud from any of us in the room, losers from all over the globe who have landed in a tourist trap because we hadn't the foresight to assure our presence in a spot of our choice.

At midnight, Jack and I stand for a few moments in San Marco, the walks jammed with onlookers, the Piazza itself open to gangs of young men carrying firecrackers and small displays of fireworks. The explosions and bursts of color coming from unexpected places unnerve us both. We turn into one of the bewildering number of small passageways and head for our hotel. I can't remember a Michigan winter this cold. In a few moments we are hopelessly lost, emerging every now and then onto the Grand Canal, then hitting a dead-end that forces us into yet another spiderweb of deserted, narrow streets. I think of the money we carry, how obvious it is that we are foreigners, how quickly we could be assaulted and pushed into the water that shines oily in the weak lamplight. "Get lost in Venice," the guidebooks urged. "Have an adventure!" Well, we were having an adventure, all right, but one we would just as soon have done without. When at last we see a sign that gives us some bearings, Jack admits that he has been frightened, too, and I find that admission a generous gift.

Back at the hotel, Jack wants to order a split of champagne with which to toast the new year. I thirst so mightily for a Coke with ice I would have traded my passport for it. While Jack negotiates with the front desk, I go to our room and in moments am under the covers, shivering, awaiting the resurrection of my toes.

In a little while Jack comes up with a small tray on which stand a large bottle of mineral water, two inches of honey-colored brandy in a snifter and miracle of miracles, my Coke with ice. I see he is as eager as I am to make it up — the blunders of the evening: the second-best dinner for which we paid far too much money, the angry words. In the end, it would be another story to laugh about when we got home. *Completo, completo.* And I think, what's a bad meal in a lifetime of breaking bread at one table?

I reach out my hand as he leans forward proffering the tray — a peace offering — and the heavy bottle of mineral water tips over, upsetting the Coke and the brandy all over me, the floor, the blankets. I grab the water bottle and try to right the two glasses, but it's too late. A swallow of Coke remains, a drop of brandy.

Jack sits silently in a little slipper chair while I mop up with a bath towel. "It's not a big deal," I tell him. I'm talking about much more than spilled brandy. His disappointment kills me; I would give my soul to ease it. I love him so much at this moment, I can feel my heart clenching and unclenching like a fist with the weight of it. I think of the man in the railroad car from Rome, how much hope we invest in the small details while the flawed world makes a mockery of the perfection we seek.

Later, we lie on our backs for a few moments in fresh white sheets starched and smelling of har-

bored sunshine, companionable, yet each of us dis-
crete, and then slowly, like old dancing partners, we
turn to one another and ease our bodies into
grooves worn familiar over the years.

Raspberry Picking

A Valedictory

Saturday morning, early, Jack and I left the still-sleeping city to gather the last of summer's raspberries. An hour later, we parked high on a hilltop of the berry farm, had our containers weighed, then walked down to where row on row of raspberry bushes sprawled near the rim of a delft-blue lake. Already the lawns were dotted with pickers: mothers and fathers, children with their little baskets, grandmothers in straw hats offering advice. We found the row assigned us, set down our trays in the rough grass and turned to the berry canes bending over with the weight of their fruit.

At first we picked furiously, lifting the prickly canes as we had been told to do, to find the fattest berries hiding underneath. We skipped the berries dried as raisins and the ones just beginning to blush. Some were so ready they fell out of reach when our clumsy fingers trembled the bushes; still, before long the bottom of my tray began to disappear.

After a while, I forgot it all, Jack and the field and the other pickers. I forgot the tray and thought only of the wonder of that morning. I straightened my body, bent like the berry canes, and I ate raspberries, ate them until I was dizzy, the buzzing wasps and I — drunk on ripe red raspberries.

Once again I turned to my picking, all the while trying to learn by heart the scent of fresh raspberries. Some winter morning, months from now, I will dip into a jar of ruby fruit, and that day will come back all of a piece: sunshine, murmuring voices, mouth and fingers sticky with juice, and the perfume of the sweetly burdened berry canes. Some winter morning, I will dip into a jam jar and taste the last of summer at the tip of a silver spoon.

—